RimRock Canyon

and "NEXT of KIN"

Published by

CLINTOONS Features

Tulsa, Oklahoma

ISBN: 0-9748849-0-1

Library of Congress Control Number: 2004090418

Rim Rock Canyon may be viewed on the Internet at:

www.rimrockcanyon.com

These **Rim Rock Canyon / Next of Kin comic strips** Appeared in Weekly and bi-weekly newspapers in the United States and Canada during 2000, 2001, 2002 and 2003.

WELCOME TO

Rim Rock Canyon & Next of Kin

For the last three and a half years, these two comic strips have been appearing in weekly and bi-weekly newspapers across the United States and even in Canada.

"Rim Rock Canyon" is a look at life on the western frontier. In *"Rim Rock Canyon"* the hope of a new life, the lure of gold, or just the lust for adventure brought together the best and the worst of humanity.

"Rim Rock Canyon" focuses on family life of Ranchers and Sodbusters, whose ability to laugh at themselves and their hardships was the key to their survival.

It is my hope that you as well will enjoy this unique humor.

"Next of Kin" features the family life of a close-knit family clan in the new Millennium.

If you enjoy these comics, I would be pleased to hear from you at my E-mail address: *clintoons@aol.com*

Also, if your area *weekly or bi-weekly newspaper* does not carry these features, please ask them to contact us at: *clintoons@aol.com*

INTRODUCTION "RIM ROCK CANYON"

AL, CAL & PAPPY BOOMER

Alvester and Lucinda Boomer loaded all their earthly belongings into a covered wagon and headed west to start a new life on the frontier. But, alas, during the first year Alvester lost his beloved wife bringing identical twin boys into the world. Alvester vowed he would raise them young'uns by the book, "The Good Book"! Alvester is known as Pappy Boomer and the twin sons named **Al and Cal.** Nobody in Rim Rock Canyon knows for sure who is who, not even ol' pappy.

JEB & JESSIE BELLE

In addition to their **many young'uns,** the family also consists of Hannible the Dog, two horses, one mule, four pigs, and a passel of chickens. Jessie Belle's mission in life is to stay one step ahead of ol'Jeb.

DESPERATE LOU

Desperate Lou is not one to sit and wait for that special "anyone" to show up. Since **Kid Cupid's** arrows don't seem to be hitting their mark, she figures that her **trusty lasso** will work better. While other people are busy chasing rainbows, she concentrates on chasing **eligible bachelors.**

THE FRONTIER DOCTOR

He has his own Hippocratic oath, "That nothing shall deter him from his appointed rounds and baby deliveries, not rain, the dark of night, or bellowing dust storms, hopefully beating his nemesis the Stork in the process. **Ol' Doc** is easy going, but sometimes loses patience with his patients.

THE OL' TIMER

The lovable Desert Rat and his mule are always searching for that **"Big Strike"!**

THE DESERT RATTLER

This is not your ordinary everyday desert Rattler, he loves people though they shun him. He confides his frustrations with his "Sidekick" **the Desert Lizard**.

INTRODUCTION "NEXT OF KIN"

Your **"BONUS FEATURE"** in this book is another comic strip **"Next of Kin".** It has appeared in weekly newspapers for the past three and a half years. The comic features a young married couple, their dog, cat, and the rest of the "close-knit" Figwell clan. This includes **Ken's Mom and Dad, Debbie's Mom** and **Uncle Obie.** No one knows for sure how old **Uncle Obie** is. To quote Ken "he's just always been there" he's not sure if he's his **Great Uncle** or **Great, Great Uncle.**

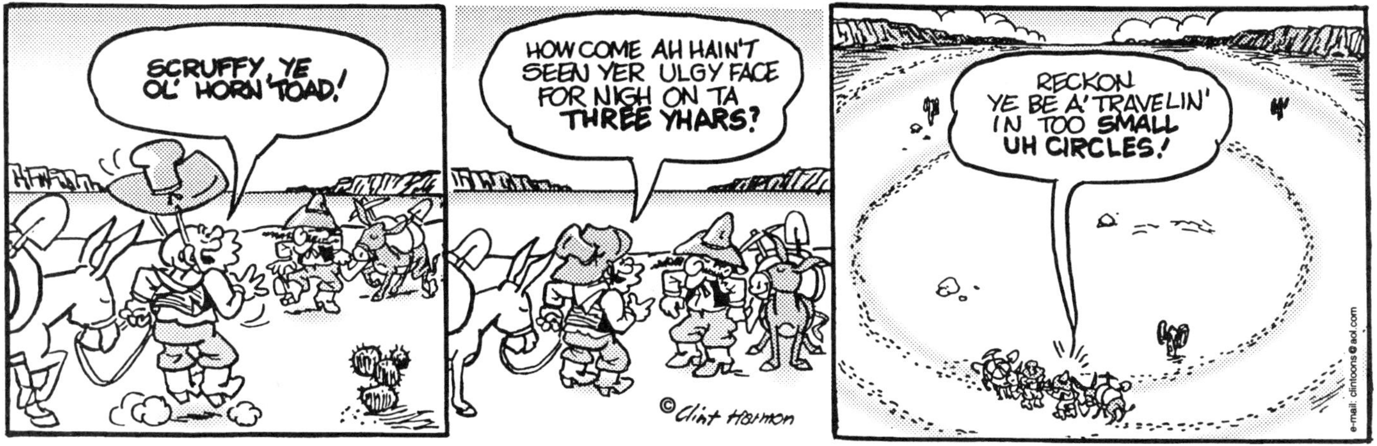
SCRUFFY, YE OL' HORN TOAD!
HOW COME AH HAIN'T SEEN YER ULGY FACE FOR NIGH ON TA **THREE YHARS?**
© Clint Harmon
RECKON YE BE A'TRAVELIN' IN TOO **SMALL UH CIRCLES!**
e-mail: clintoons@aol.com

WHUT'S OUR MULES UP TO SCRUFFY?
HEE HAW!
HEE HAW!
HEE HAW!
RECKON THEY BE A'SWAPPIN' FUNNY STORIES!
HEE HAW!
HEE HAW!
HEE HAW!
e-mail: clintoons@aol.com
'BOUT US?
YUP!
HEE HAW!
HEE HAW!
HEE HAW!
HEE HAW!
HEE HAW!
HEE HAW!
HEE HAW!
HEE HAW!
HEE HAW!
THUMP!
THUMP!
THUMP!
THUMP!
© Clint Harmon

TIZ SAID THAT LOVE IS BUT LIFE SET TO MUSIC!
AH DON'T WANT TO CHANGE TH' ARRANGEMENT...
© Clint Harmon
AH JUST WANTS TO SING A'LONG!
UH OH!!
e-mail: clintoons@aol.com
THERE GOES THE NEIGHBORHOOD!
© Clint Harmon

WHEN YE GETS TO FEELING LOW JEB... JUST COUNT...
...YUR BLESSINGS!
AH THINK THET BE MY PROBLEM PARSON!
...WE BEEN BLESSED TOO MUCH!
Clint Harmon

LOOK PA. LOOK!...
... HE FOLLOWED ME HOME!...CAN AH KEEP HIM PA? PLEASE PA. CAN AH? PLEASE PA, PLEASE!
ONLY IF'IN YE PUTS HIM ON UH LEASH SO'S HE WON'T CHASE TH' CHICKENS!
©
Clint Harmon

HEY YOU'RE BACK. I THOUGHT YOU WAS GOING DOMESTIC!
HEY. I LET 'EM PUT A LEASH ON ME...
AN' I EVEN WENT ALONG WITH THAT "FETCH TH' STICK" ROUTINE.. BUT...
...I DRAWS TH' LINE AT COON HUNTING!
Clint Harmon

TSK, TSK FEISTY YOUNG'UNS!
AL AN' CAL TH' IDENTICAL TWINS WON'T BE SO IDENTICAL AFTER THET FRACAS!
BOP!
SOK!
WOP!
YE BE FORGETTIN' THET PAPPY BOOMER...
...RAISED THEM BOYS BY TH' EYE FER AN EYE AN' UH TOOTH FER UH TOOTH RULE!
Clint Harmon

THIS'N WILL DO JUST FINE. AH'LL TAKE IT!
DOOR TO DOOR GEN. STORE
Clint Harmon
GOOD CHOICE JEB, THAT NET WILL HOLD ANY CATFISH IN TH' TERRITORY!
CATCH ME ANOTHER'N PA, AH BE'BOUT DONE WITH THIS'N!

I DON'T GET IT, WHAT'S WRONG WITH ME? WHY DON'T FOLKS LIKE ME?
I THINK I KNOW...
...THEY GETS RATTLED AROUND YOU!
HEY. THAT'S TH' WAY I SAY HOWDY!
Clint Harmon

TSK,TSK, HOW PATHETIC! POOR BOY!
YOUNG FELLER YOU WON'T CATCH ANYTHING THAR!
YEAH, THEY SHORE HAIN'T BITING!...
... BUT YE OUGHTA BEEN HYAR THIS MORNING!
Clint Harmon

GOTCHA!
SNAP!
DANG! HE LOOKED LIKE HE'D MEASURE UP TO MY STRICT REQUIREMENTS FOR MATRIMONIAL PURPOSES!
RIGHT, BODY TEMPERTURE 98.6!
Clint Harmon

WHUT DO YE EXPECT TO ACCOMPLISH...
...LAYIN' ON THET PORCH ALL TH' TIME?
Clint Harmon
WHOA THAR!
...YE MEAN TA SAY THAT THEM LONG TRIPS 'ROUND TH' SUN EVER' YEAR DON'T COUNT!!

AH, ME GORGEOUS L'IL CACTUS BLOSSOM WHERE HAVE YE BEEN ALL MY LIFE?
POOF!
Clint Harmon
DANG!! AH ALWAYS WAKES UP BEFORE TH' HANKY PANKY!

YE BOYS SHOULDN'T BE A' BEATIN' UP ON ONE UH' TUTHER BEIN' **BROTHERS AN' ALL!**
?
?
HE'S RIGHT! THIS'S JUST AS MUCH FUN!
AN' IT DON'T HURT NONE!
Clint Harmon

WHOA!
OOOOOOW!
IT'S, AT TIMES LIKE THIS THAT I MISS **TREES** TH' **MOST!**
?
Clint Harmon

JUST LISTEN TO THET OL' COYOTE A'HOWLIN', THET'S TH' WAY HE FINDS UH MATE!
OOOW!
Clint Harmon

LOOK!
EEEEE!!
WE'VE WONDERED INTO HOSTILE SAVAGE COUNTRY!
Clint Harmon

JAIL
Clint Harmon
WHAAA!
HAH!
TH' STORK BEAT YE AGAIN, DOC!

I'M ONLINE AND READY FOR HITS WITH MY VERY OWN WEBSITE!
OL' DAD WOULD BE SO PROUD IF HE COULD ONLY SEE ME NOW!
HE ALWAYS SAID "SON BUILD YOUR WEB...
...WHERE IT'S LEAST LIKELY TO BE DISTURBED!
Clint Harmon

HAH. I CAME ALL THE WAY FROM NEW YORK TO WRITE ABOUT THE ROMANTIC WILD WEST...
SALOON
Clint Harmon
WHEN DO I SEE SOME ACTION?
SALOON
JAIL
ANY MINUTE NOW!
BENEATH TH' COWBOYS VEST BEATS MANY BRAVE YOUNG HEARTS!
BUT, WHEN INTO TOWN RIDES "DESPERATE LOU," ALL THEIR COURAGE SOON DEPARTS!
PA, HE SAYS HE'S CAL AN' AH'M AL, BUT REALLY HE'S AL AN' AH BE CAL!
DON'T YE YOUNG'UN'S FRET NONE, YER OL' PAPPY'LL HANDLE THIS!
Clint Harmon

MY READERS BACK EAST ARE ANXIOUS TO READ TH' STORY OF TH' BRAVE FRONTIER SHERIFF!
A MAN TO WHOM HIS FELLOW CITIZENS GAVE THEIR VOTE OF CONFIDENCE! A MAN THAT PUT LAW AND ORDER ABOVE HIS OWN SAFETY! **RIGHT?**
NOT EXACTLY...
Clint Harmon
PRESS
...AH JUST GOT TH' **SHORT STRAW!**
DOC, AH SURE APPRECIATES TH' GREAT JOB YER DOIN'! **KEEP UP TH' GOOD WORK!**
WHAP!
AH, A GREAT STORY FOR MY READERS BACK EAST!
DOC, DOESN'T IT WARM YOUR HEART FOR A FELLOW CITIZEN TO **SAY THAT?**
IT WOULD IF HE WARN'T TH' LOCAL **UNDERTAKER!**
JAIL
GENERAL STORE
Clint Harmon

SHERIFF, AH WOULD LIKE TO GO AFTER THIS DISGUSTING VARMENT!
REWARD
RECKON YE BE AFTER TH' REWARD, EH DESPERATE LOU?
SHUCKS NO, AH BE THINKING MORE LIKE...
Clint Harmon
...FINDERS KEEPERS!
REWARD

DANG! LOOKS LIKE DOC'S GONNA BEAT ME THIS TIME!
NOT ONLY AM I FIGHTING A STRONG HEADWIND, BUT...
...THEY ORDERED DOUBLE THIS TIME!
Clint Harmon

AH BE PLUMB PUT OUT WITH YE JEB!
JUST WHUT'S IT GONNA TAKE TO GET YE UP OFF'IN THET PORCH?
?
Clint Harmon
...TH' REPEAL OF TH' LAW OF GRAVITY?

THOSE ARE VOWELS, NOW WHO CAN GIVE US TWO EXAMPLES OF A CONSONANT?
a e
i o
u
ALRIGHT, AL OR CAL WHICHEVER YE BE!
PAPPY SAYS WE BOTH BE UH CONSTANT PAIN IN TH' BACKSIDE!
Clint Harmon

ROSES 'ER RED!
DAFFODILS 'ER YELLER!
AH'M GONNA CATCH ME UH FELLER!
Clint Harmon

BINGO!
YE DON'T WANT ME LOU, I'M ALREADY MARRIED AN' I'VE GOT THREE YOUNG'UN'S!
Clint Harmon
IT'S JUST LIKE FISHIN', YE GOTTA TOSS 'EM BACK IF THAR NOT LEGAL!

I'M PLAGUED WITH A BAD REPUTATION, BUT I'M REALLY A PUSSYCAT!...
...FOR EXAMPLE...
SOME FOLKS HERE 'BOUTS ARE SO HARD UP THEY CAN'T AFFORD STORE BOUGHT RATTLES FOR THEIR WEE YOUNG'UNS!
RATTLE
RATTLE!
Clint Harmon

?!
GREAT DIRECTIONS: THAT WAY TO THE SECOND MIRAGE AND MAKE A LEFT!
Clint Harmon

WHUT BE THET THING UP YOUNDER?
OH THAT!
DOOR TO DOOR GEN. STORE
...AS OF RIGHT NOW ONLY A FEW AFFLUENT PEOPLE UP EAST HAVE ONE OF THOSE SORT OF A STATUS SYMBOL!
GOLLYEE! AH'LL TAKE IT! WHAT'S IT FUR?
THUNDERATION!... YE MEAN THEM FOLKS HAVE IN-HOUSE OUTHOUSES?
Clint Harmon

YER MA ©☆!! MUTT ATE ALL MY CHOPPED LIVER CATFISH BAIT!
THUNDERATION HANNIBLE! WHUT DO YE HAVE TO SAY FER YERSELF?
ASK HIM DO HE HAVE A BROMO-SELTZER?
Clint Harmon

MIND IF I ASK YOU A PERSONAL QUESTION?
NOT AT ALL!
DON'T YOU EVER GET TIRED OF LEFTOVERS?
Clint Harmon

WHO BE TH' YOUNG FELLER DOWNLOADIN' FROM TH' STAGE, DOC?
OH, THET BE RIMROCK'S NEW LAWYER, "MR. WRIGHT!"
SALOON
DOC, DID YE SAY MR. RIGHT?
RIGHT!
YAHOO!
AH BE A'WAITIN' FER THET FELLER UH LONG TIME!
SALOON
Clint Harmon

HOWDY, CARE FOR A LITTLE DRAW POKER? I JUST HAPPEN TO HAVE A FULL SET OF TH' TOOLS OF MY TRADE!
FLIP! FLIP!
AH THOUGHT YER TRADE BE PRACTICED IN UH SALOON!
NORMALLY, BUT I VACATED MY LAST PRACTICE TO TAKE ADVANTAGE OF AN OFFER THAT I JUST COULDN'T REFUSE!
SURE YE MADE TH' RIGHT DECISION?
POSITIVE!!
TAKE A HIKE OR HANG!
Clint Harmon
LOOK! INJUNS!
BEST LET ME HANDLE THIS, WITH INDIANS TH' GREETING IS VERY, VERY IMPORTANT!
HOW!
HOWDY!!
Clint Harmon

I'VE NEVER BAGGED UH BIRD OF THIS BULK BEFORE...
WHAT'S TH' BEST WAY TO CLEAN A TURKEY?
PERSONALLY I PREFER DRAW POKER WITH TH' DEUCES AND JOKER WILD!
AH HATES TO BE UH HUNTING PARTY POOPER BUT THAT'S NO TURKEY YE HAVE THERE.
?
?
...IT'S A TURKEY BUZZARD!
CLOSE ENOUGH!

GIVE ME A MAN, JUST A MAN, 'CAUSE AH HATES BEIN' SINGLE! AH JUST WANTS TO HEAR THEM WEDDING BELLS JINGLE!
AH'D GIVE MY PEARL HANDLE SIX SHOOTER AN' BUFFALO HIDE HOLSTER IF MR. RIGHT ER WRONG WOULD COME TROTTIN' UP HYAR, RIGHT NOW!
AN I'D GIVE MY NEXT SIX WEEKS RATION OF OATS FOR A PAIR OF EARPLUGS, RIGHT NOW!
OOOOW!!

YE PASSED TH' TEST SETH! YE DON'T NEED SPECS!
THUNDERATION, THEN HOW COME AH BE PLAGUED WITH VISION PROBLEMS?
OFTEN?
HMM!...
OH, OFF N' ON. WHUT DO YE PRESCRIBE FER ME, DOC?
... UH SIZE SMALLER HAT!

HOO HAW, BEGINNER'S LUCK! AH HAS WON TH' LAST THREE POTS!
OL' TIMER, YOU GOT TO MOVE YOUR MULE!
I'M NOT MAKING ANY ACCUSATIONS, BUT THERE'S BEEN ALTOGETHER TOO MUCH EYE BATTIN', HEAD NODDIN' AND EAR TWITCHIN' GOING ON AROUND HERE!
Clint Harmon

JACOB, BENJAMIN, CHRISTOPHER, OR WHOEVER YE BE, COME HYAR!
AH BE EDGAR MA!
WAL EDGAR, GO AN SHOO TH' CHICKENS OFF YER PA!!
HE BEEN A'LAYIN' IN THET ONE POSITION SO LONG...
...THEY THINK HE BE UH OL' SACK UH FEED!
Clint Harmon

FOLKS ARE ALWAYS WONDERIN' WHY AH DON'T RETIRE!
THUNDERATION! THEY OR'TA KNOW THAT...
... AH CAN'T GO INTO RETIREMENT TILL JEB'S OL' LADY GOES INTO MENOPAUSE!
Clint Harmon

RUMBLE!
THET DOES IT! NO MATTER HOW SHE BEGS WITH THEM BIG BROWN EYES AN' LAID BACK EARS...
Clint Harmon
... NO MORE SHARING MY BEANS WITH 'ER !!

YE DIDN'T FIX TH' HEN HOUSE ROOF! OH WELL,
THAT'S ABOUT WHUT AH EXPECTED!
THAT'S GOOD!
Clint Hamon
AH LIKES TO KEEP HER EXPECTATION LEVEL LOW...
'CAUSE "SIGH"
AH SURE HATES TO SEE THAT WOMAN DISAPPOINTED!
IF AH CAN'T GET YE UP OFF 'IN THET PORCH..
Clint Hamon
...LEAST WAYS MOVE UH LITTLE NOW AN' AGAIN, YER BEGINNING TO ATTRACT ATTENTION!
HEH, HEH. SILLY WOMAN HAIN'T UH SOUL IN MILES O' HYAR!

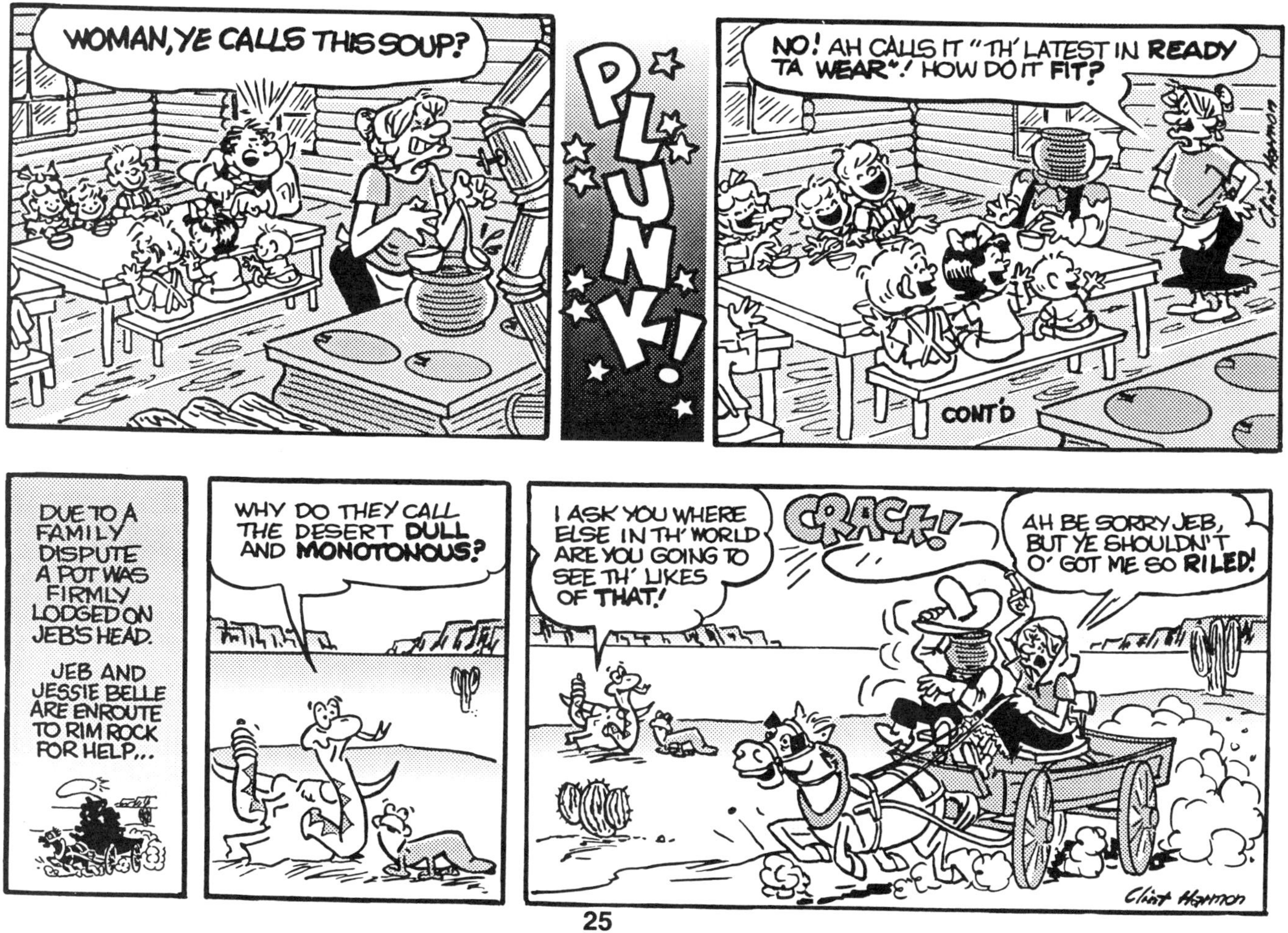
WOMAN, YE CALLS THIS SOUP?
PLUNK!
NO! AH CALLS IT "TH' LATEST IN READY TA WEAR"! HOW DO IT FIT?
CONT'D
DUE TO A FAMILY DISPUTE A POT WAS FIRMLY LODGED ON JEB'S HEAD.
JEB AND JESSIE BELLE ARE ENROUTE TO RIM ROCK FOR HELP...
WHY DO THEY CALL THE DESERT DULL AND MONOTONOUS?
I ASK YOU WHERE ELSE IN TH' WORLD ARE YOU GOING TO SEE TH' LIKES OF THAT!
CRACK!
AH BE SORRY JEB, BUT YE SHOULDN'T O' GOT ME SO RILED!
Clint Harmon

DUE TO A FAMILY DISPUTE A POT WAS FIRMLY LODGED ON JEB'S HEAD.
JEB AND JESSIE BELLE ARE ENROUTE TO RIM ROCK FOR HELP...
NO BABIES, SHOOT OUTS ER EPIDEMICS, YE THINK MY PRACTICE BE A'GOIN' TO **POT** PARSON?
SOONER THAN YE BE A' THINKIN' DOC!
SALOON
JAIL
GENERAL STORE
Clint Harmon

DUE TO A DISPUTE WITH JESSIE BELLE A POT WAS FIRMLY LODGED ON JEB'S HEAD!
DOC IS NOW TRYING TO GET IT OFF!
UGH, STUCK TIGHTER'N UH 500 LB. SOW IN UH HOG WOLLER!
OOOOH! KIN YE GET IT **OFF? YE JUS' GOTTA GET IT OFF!!**
NOW, NOW, CALM YERSELF MADAM, WE'LL GET IT OFF ONE WAY ER TUTHER!
OOOH, DOC AH HOPES SO!
Clint Harmon
AH BE A'USIN' THET POT AT LEAST **THREE TIMES UH WEEK!**

DUE TO A DISPUTE WITH JESSIE BELLE A POT WAS FIRMLY LODGED ON JEB'S HEAD!
DOC IS NOW TRYING TO GET IT OFF!
WHUT'S HE SAYIN' DOC? WHUT'S HE SAYIN?
SIZZLE!
NOTHIN' AH BE REPEATIN' IN TH' COMPANY OF WOMEN FOLK ER SMALL CHILDREN!
Clint Hammon

DUE TO A DISPUTE WITH JESSIE BELLE A POT WAS FIRMLY LODGED ON JEB'S HEAD!
DOC IS NOW TRYING TO GET IT OFF!
THAR BE ONLY ONE THING AH HAVEN'T TRIED, IT'S UH MITE RISKY, BUT IT BE OUR ONLY HOPE OUTSIDE O' AMPUTATION!
LATER
LOOK OUT! IT'S A U.F.P!
UNIDENTIFIED FLYING POT!
GEN STORE
JAIL
WOOSH!
ACK CHOO!
TOMORROW "POT LUCK"
Clint Hammon

EPILOGUE
DOC DEVISES A LAST DITCH PLAN TO REMOVE THE POT THAT IS STUCK ON JEB'S HEAD...
BORROWING THE SMITHY'S BELLOWS HE USES IT TO FORCE PEPPER UNDER THE POT'S RIM...
SUCCESS AT LAST!
ACK CHOO!
HAH. WORKED GREAT...
EDITOR'S NOTE: DON'T TRY THIS AT HOME!
Clint Harmon
..'CEPT MAYBE UH MITE TOO MUCH PEPPER!
DOC HAS JUST REMOVED THE POT THAT WAS STUCK ON JEB'S HEAD...
THAR YE BE MADAM YUR VERY OWN LOVIN' HUBBY MINUS POT!
SOUNDS LIKE OL' JEB JUS' GOT HIS SECOND WIND!
Clint Harmon
PUT TH' POT BACK ON DOC!

EVERYDAY SINCE I'VE BEEN THE SUBSTITUTE TEACHER I'VE HAD TO KEEP YOU TWO AFTER SCHOOL!
SCHOOL
YOU BOYS MUST BE A GLUTTON FOR PUNISHMENT!
SCHOOL
NO MA'AM, WE DESARVES THIS PUNISHMENT!...WE BEEN BAAAAD BOYS!
Clint Harmon

MY, AREN'T WE THE HAPPY ONE TODAY!
WITH GOOD REASON!
A COWBOY LOST ALL HIS GEAR ESCAPING DESPERATE LOU'S LASSO!
...AND NOW I'VE GOT A BUDDY!!
THOUGH, HE'S NOT BIG ON SMALL TALK!
Clint Harmon

KEERFUL THAR 'BOUT PETTIN' OL HANNIBLE!
WHY, UNCLE JEB, DO HE BITE?
NAW, BUT YE BE IN FER UH SEVERE...
...TONGUE LASHING!
Clint Harmon

STILL NO WORD FROM TH' TERRITORIAL JUDGE ON YER APPEAL, NOZZLENOSE...
GENERAL STORE
BUT WE GOTTA POSTPONE YUR HANGING ANYWAY!
...THET ROPE'S BECOMING TOO FRAYED!
"NO NOOSE IS GOOD NOOSE!"
Clint Harmon

IF FATE HAD ONLY BEEN KINDER TO ME, I BELIEVE I COULD HAVE ACHIEVED GREATNESS!
?
WHAT DO YOU THINK??
HMMM...
I THINK YOU ARE LITERALLY AND FIGURATIVELY... OUT OF YOUR SKULL!

QUIT YER INFERNAL COMPLAININ' JEB!
YE BRINGED IT ALL ON YERSELF...
IF 'IN AH'VE TOLD YE ONCE AH'VE TOLD YE UH THOUSAND TIMES...
...FIX TH' LEAK IN TH' HEN HOUSE ROOF!

QUITE'CHA NAGGIN' WOMAN, AN JUS' BE THANKFUL I'M NOT UH COUCH POTATO!
YE GOT THET RIGHT! YUR NO COUCH POTATO!
... MORE LIKE UH PORCH SQUASH!

AW SUGAR, WHY SO SHY?
Chet Harmon
AAAAAAAAAAAAAAAA!
WHUMP!
WHUMP!
SNAP!
SIGH!
TIZ' BETTER TO HAVE LOVED AND LOST THAN TO HAVE NEVER LOVED AT ALL!

AH'VE HEARD TELL THET FER EVERY MAN THAR'S A WOMAN AN' FER EVERY WOMAN THAR'S A MAN...
IF THET BE TRUE...
WHAR'S MINE!

MANY THANKS FER WHUT WE AIR ABOUT TA RECIEVE AN' GOD BLESS US EVERYONE!
... AND LORD YOU KNOW THET BE UH PASSEL 'O BLESSINGS!

SERIOUSLY, IF FATE HAD DELT ME A BETTER HAND OR HANDS, I COULD HAVE BECOME A GREAT ACTOR!
TIZ' SUCH A SHAME TO WASTE A GREAT TALENT!
TALENT! WHAT TALENT?
..ALAS POOR YORIK, I KNEW HIM WELL!

AH'M CHECKIN' YUR HEART RATE SETH!
KNOCK YURSELF OUT DOC!
OH NO! TH' OL' TICKER JUST UP AN' STOPPED!
AARRG! MY HEART STOPPED??
NO. MY WATCH!
WHEW!

I WANT MY READERS BACK EAST TO KNOW WHAT IT TAKES TO BE A DOCTOR ON TH' FRONTIER!
GENERAL STORE
THAT'S EASY! TO BE SUCCESSFUL IT TAKES **TWO THINGS!**
SALOON
JAIL
GENERAL STORE
BABIES N' BULLETS!

SINCE YOUR A'GOING THERE ANYWAYS. WOULD YOU **DROP THIS OFF AT JEB'S PLACE?**
Happy Holidays

AAHHH! NEW YEAR'S DAY! UH WHOLE DAY OF JUST REST N' RELAXATION!
HAH! HAIN'T THAT YUR AGENDA FER EVERY DAY IN TH' WEEK!
YEAH! BUT, HOLIDAYS 'ER GUILT FREE!

IF YE BOYS AIR A' GOIN' TA SCHOOL WHUT BE TH' PACK MULE FER?
LUNCH!

HEH! HEH! PAPPY BOOMER'S IDENTICAL TWIN YOUNG'UNS ARE AT IT AGAIN!
BOP!
SOK!
WOP!
AH'M GONNA STOMP TH' WADDIN' OUT O' YE AL!
YE IDJET! I'M CAL! YUR AL!
WHATEVER!
PRAISE BE! TH' DROUTH BE BROKEN!
HOO BOY!
ROAR!
RUMBLE!
KABLAM!
CRASH!
HOO BOY!

YE BE IN FER A RARE TREAT THAR SCRUFFY! THET'S MAH SECRET RECIPE FER...
FOOM!
JALAPEÑO PANCAKES!
HEE HAW! HEE HAW!
THERE, THERE, LI'L FELLOW, AH FEELS YUR PAIN!...
PURR! PURR!
...YUR ALWAYS ON TH' OUTSIDE, LOOKIN IN!
WELCOME TO TH' CLUB!
PURRR!
PURR!

I SHOT AN ARROW IN THE AIR...
Z'NG!
...IT FELL TO EARTH I KNOW NOT WHERE!
I THINK THET BE A BIG PART OF MY PROBLEM RIGHT THERE!

HANNIBLE!
BAD DOG!! WHEN AIR YE GONNA LEARN THET...
...CHASING CHICKENS IS NOT UH RECOGNIZED SPORT!

JEB, AH BE ANXIOUS TA KNOW WHUT YE THINK O' MY ORIGINAL RECIPE FER RABBIT RAVIOLI!
LORD, PLEASE GIVE ME TH' WISDOM TA MAKE TH' RIGHT DECISION WHETHER...
TO UPSET MY STOMACH OR TO UPSET JESSIE BELLE!

IT BE TIME FER YER EYE TEST SETH!
DOC. AH DON'T PUT A LOT OF STORE IN YER EYE TEST!
WHY SETH?
WAL FER ONE THING!
...WHOEVER MADE THET EYE CHART COULDN"T SPELL WORTH A HOOT!
VRQLNP
SQJPXF

SCRUFFY. YE BE WORRYIN' WAY TOO MUCH ABOUT BEING IN HOSTILE INJUN COUNTRY!
11/30-12/6
©2003 Clint Harmon Email: clintoons@aol.com
HAH! THET BE EASY FER YE TO SAY!
AH GOT A LOT MORE TO LOSE THAN YE!

IT WARN'T ME PAPPY! IT WAR AL! I'M CAL!
???
3/17-23
www.rimrockcanyon.com
Email: clintoons@aol.com
AH BE A'GIVIN' YE YOUNG'UN'S FAIR WARNING! IT'S AGONNA BE "BIG TIME WOODSHED"...
... IF'N AH EVER FINDS OUT WHICH ONE O' YE TWIN RASCALS BE AL!
©2002 Clint Harmon Dist.by Clintoons Features

WHY DO THEY CALL YE QUICK CHANGE?
TOSS UP A QUARTER!
PING!
BLAM!
ZIP!
©2002 Clint Harmon Dist.by Clintoons Features
TWO DIMES AN UH NICKEL!
Email: clintoons@aol.com
www.rimrockcanyon.com
3/31-4/6

AH FISHIN', WHAR YE CAN ENJOY PEACEFUL RELAXATION WHILE COMMUNICATING WITH NATURE!
3/24-30
©2002 Clint Harmon Dist.by Clintoons Features
HOWEVER, THERE DO HAPPEN TO BE ONE DOWNSIDE.
www.rimrockcanyon.com Email: clintoons@aol.com
TOO MANY INTERRUPTIONS!

MAKING DECISIONS IS TOUGH!
NAW. IT'S EASY...
4/21-27
Email: clintoons@aol.com
©2002 Clint Harmon
IF IT DOESN'T SMELL GOOD ENOUGH TO EAT...
OR BAD ENOUGH TO ROLL IN ...
Dist.by Clintoons Features
DOUSE IT!
WORKS FOR ME!

SHERIFF, AH DON'T THINK THAT IT'S UH GOOD IDEA FER JEB TO JOIN YER POSSE!
©2002 Clint Harmon
BUT JESSIE BELLE, IT BE MY DUTY AS AN' UPSTANDING CITIZEN!
4/1-13
HAW! YE NEVER BE UPSTANDING! 'SIDES YER CARRYIN' TOO MUCH LEAD AROUND IN YER CABOOSE AS TIZ.!
Email: clintoons@aol.com

TH' DESERT IS SO BARREN!
YEAH!
©2002 Clint Harmon Dist.by Clintoons Features
SO LONELY!
YEAH!
4/14-20
SO DEAD!
YEAH!
Email: clintoons@aol.com

NO CARDS FOR ME, I'LL JUST PLAY THESE!
IT'S ALL YOURS! I'M OUT'TA HERE!
IT'S "DESPERATE LOU"!
Email: clintoons@aol.com
4/28-5/4
SHOOT! I TO BLUFFED HIM OUT TH' GAME!
©2002 Clint Harmon
PREPARE TO MEET YOUR PREACHER!
CLICK!
CONTINUED NEXT WEEK!

YOU DON'T WANT ME LOU! I'VE GOT HALITOSIS, DANDRUFF AND INGROWN TOENAILS!
5/5-11
REJOICE! THIS BE YOUR LUCKY DAY!
Email: clintoons@aol.com
AH HAIN'T PICKY!
©2002 Clint Harmon
Dist.by Clintoons Features

ASK 'EM PA!
HOWDY! WHUT DOES TH' SMOKE MEAN?
©2002 Clint Harmon
Email: clintoons@aol.com
HMM!
SOMEBODY BURN'UM BEANS!
5/19-25

OOOOW!
5/12 -18
©2002 Clint Harmon
Dist.by Clintoons Features
YE BRINGED IT ALL ON YERSELF **HANNIBLE!** WHEN AIR YE GONNA LEARN THET...
CACTUS HAIN'T **"USER FRIENDLY"!**
Email: clintoons@aol.com

YAHOO!
YIPEEE!
Email: clintoons@aol.com
©2002 Clint Harmon
Dist.by Clintoons Features

SO, YE CAN JUST FORGET IT, IF YE DON'T SLOP TH' HOGS, FEED TH' CHICKENS AN' GATHER TH' EGGS!
AW. JESSIE BELLE! THET BE CRUEL AND UNUSUAL PUNISHMENT!
©2002 Clint Harmon
SHE BE A'HOLDIN' TH' POT ROAST HOSTAGE!
Email: clintoons@aol.com
6/2-8

IS THIS WHAR YE GETS LICENSES FER MARRYIN' UP?
YUP!
Email: clintoons@aol.com
WHO'S TH' OTHER PARTY?
OH. JUST LEAVE THET PART BLANK!
©2002 Clint Harmon
6/9-15
WHEN AH FINDS TH' OTHER PARTY, AH DON'T WANT TO WASTE TIME ON PAPER WORK!

YAAAAAAAAA!!
WHEN I RATTLE AT FOLKS I AM JUST BEING FRIENDLY!
6/16-22
SIGH!
I LIKE PEOPLE BUT PEOPLE DON'T LIKE ME!
Email: clintoons@aol.com
Dist.by Clintoons Features
I RECKON YER JUST A PUSSYCAT TRAPPED IN THE BODY OF A RATTLESNAKE!
©2002 Clint Harmon

YE BE FIT AS A FIDDLE CY!
HOWEVER ...
©2002 Clint Harmon Dist.by Clintoons Features
YER HOSS NEEDS TO LOSE SOME WEIGHT!
Email: clintoons@aol.com
6/23-29

PARSON, WHUT DO YE THINK OF TH' "BIG BANG" THEORY?
©2002 Clint Harmon Email: clintoons@aol.com
IF THAR WAS A "BIG BANG"...
6/30-7/6
I RECKON WE KNOW WHO WAS IN CHARGE OF TH' FIREWORKS!
AMEN!
BANG!
BOOM!

DID YOU COME OUT WEST TO START A NEW LIFE?
YUP!
©2002 Clint Harmon
ARE THE LOCAL INDIANS FRIENDLY?
YUP!
DO YOU HAVE ANY LIVESTOCK?
YUP!
Email: clintoons@aol.com Dist.by Clintoons Features
I BET YOU THINK I'M AN IDIOT FOR INTERVIEWING SOMEONE WHO NEVER SAYS ANYTHING BUT "YUP"?
YUP!
7/1-13

RECKON WE BE GOIN' NOW LUKE!
WAIT! IS THIS'IN ONE O' YOUR'IN OR ONE O' OUR'IN?
GEE, I DON'T RIGHTLY KNOW!
DUNK HIM IN TH' RAIN BARREL LUKE. HE BEEN PLAYIN' IN TH' HOG WALLOW!
©2002 Clint Harmon
Email: clintoons@aol.com
7/14-20

HOW, PULL UP A ROCK AN' JOIN TH' GAME!
©2002 Clint Harmon
BETTER YET, JOIN US TONIGHT FOR A GAME AT MY TEE PEE!
GREAT! BLACKJACK OR POKER?
7/21-27
Dist.by Clintoons Features
Email: clintoons@aol.com
BINGO!

EVERYBODY SHUNS ME, NOBODY WANTS TO BE MY FRIEND!
I'LL BE YOUR FRIEND!
©2002 Clint Harmon
Email: clintoons@aol.com
YOU WILL?
SURE! NOW GIVE US A BIG HUG!
7/28 – 8/3
SORRY, NO ARMS!
WHEW!

KEEP YOUR EYES PEELED SHOTGUN. WE BE IN DANGEROUS COUNTRY!
HOLD UP!!
WHOA!
©2002 Clint Harmon Email: clintoons@aol.com
YE STRUCK OUT AGAIN DESPERATE LOU, HAIN'T NO ELIGIBLE BACHELORS ABOARD!
8/4 – 10

HOLD STILL EDGAR, AH'VE ONLY GOT **TH' FIRST LAYER OFF!**
BATH TIME BE TH' **BADDEST TIME!**
©2002 Clint Harmon
Email: clintoons@aol.com
HOWEVER!
TH' **GOOD TIMES** MORE THAN MAKE UP FOR TH' **BAD 'UN'S**
?

ANY ACHES ER PAINS, JESSIE BELLE?
ONE **BIG PAIN** DOC, BUT YE CAN'T HELP ME!
©2002 Clint Harmon
WHERE MIGHT THIS **PAIN** BE JESSIE BELLE?
A'STANDIN' RIGHT THAR!
Email: clintoons@aol.com

YER EXCUSE ALL SUMMER WAS TH' DRY SPELL!
©2002 Clint Harmon Email: clintoons@aol.com
NOW, YER EXCUSE IS, IT'S RAINING!
8/25-31
SO, WHEN AIR YE GONNA FIX TH' ROOF?
A QUARRELSOME WIFE IS LIKE A CONSTANT DRIPPING ON A RAINY DAY; PROVERBS 27:15

HELP!
HELP!
SOMEBODY PLEASE...
©2002 Clint Harmon Email: clintoons@aol.com
...SHOOT ME!
9/1-7

AL AN' CAL BOOMER ARE SO BIG AN' ALL, HOW DO THEY GET ALONG WITH TH' SMALLER CHILDREN?
SCHOOL
JUST GREAT, PARSON!
©2002 Clint Harmon
IN FACT, THEY CAN HARDLY WAIT FOR RECESS SO THEY CAN PLAY WITH AL N' CAL!
9/8-14
Email: clintoons@aol.com

DIG IN THAR SCRUFFY, THAT BE MY SECRET RECIPE FER DESERT STEW!
9/15-21
HEY!! THIS TASTE JUST LIKE MOM USE'TA MAKE!!
WOW! THAT GOOD HUH?
©2002 Clint Harmon
Email: clintoons@aol.com
NO! THAT BAD, THAT'S TH' REASON I LEFT HOME!

HOW DID YE GET TO BE A NEWSPAPER REPORTER?
BY STUDYING JOURNALISM AT A UNIVERSITY BACK EAST. HOW WAS YOU EDUCATED?
BY STUDYING TH' MAIL ORDER CATALOG AT A LITTLE HOUSE ON TH' PRAIRIE!
9/22-28
Email: clintoons@aol.com
©2002 Clint Harmon

SMACK!
?
9/29-10/5
HOW KIN YE STAY MAD AT A GUY LIKE THET?
HEH. HEH SHE'S SOOO CUTE WHEN SHE'S ANGRY!
©2002 Clint Harmon Email: clintoons@aol.com

WHOA! NOT GOOD!
WHUT AH NEEDS IS A FEW GOOD HANDS!
SHOOT! I'D SETTLE FOR JUST TWO GOOD HANDS!
10/6-12
©2002 Clint Harmon Email: clintoons@aol.com

YOUR BLAMED DOG ATE ALL O' MY CATFISH STINK BAIT!
ALRIGHT HANNIBLE! WHUT DO YE HAV' TO SAY TO THET?
10/13-19
©2002 Clint Harmon Email: clintoons@aol.com
I'VE 'AD BETTER!

HANNIBLE, DO YE PROMISE ME THAT YOU'LL NEVER CHASE TH' CHICKENS AGAIN?
UH HUH!
Email: clintoons@aol.com
©2002 Clint Harmon
YEAH, I KNOW I PROMISED,
BUT...
Dist.by Clintoons Features
THEY LET SLEEPING DOGS LIE DON'T THEY?
10/20–26

PAPPY, I JUST GOTTA COMMEND YE ON TH' BEHAVIOR O' YUR YOUNG'UN'S AL AN' CAL!
10/27–11/2
WAL, THANK YE DOC!
©2002 Clint Harmon Dist.by Clintoons Features
HOWEVER, IT TOOK A MITE O' DOIN'!
Email: clintoons@aol.com

HE LOVES ME!
HE LOVES ME NOT!
HE LOVES ME!
HE LOVES ME NOT!
HE LOVES ME!
©2002 Clint Harmon
Email: clintoons@aol.com
WAIT A MINUTE! WHO IS HE? AN' WHAR IS HE?
TOY WITH ME WILL YE?

I LIKE PEOPLE!
Email: clintoons@aol.com
BUT PEOPLE DON'T LIKE ME!
©2002 Clint Harmon Dist.by Clintoons Features
HEY! WE GOT A LOT IN COMMON!

YE KNOW SCRUFFY, AH DON'T KNOW WHY FOLKS WOULD WANT TO LIVE ANYWHAR ELSE!
11/17-23
WE HAVE IT ALL RIGHT HERE! TH' BEAUTIFUL BUTTES, TH' MAJESTIC CACTUS, TH' PURPLY SAGE AND
AND COFFEE IN TH' POT NINE DAYS OLD!
PTUI!
©2002 Clint Harmon
Email: clintoons@aol.com

I AM THANKFUL THAT I AM A MAJESTIC FOWL, NAMELY "A WILD TURKEY"
Email: clintoons@aol.com
BUT YOU, A LOWLY RATTLESNAKE, WHAT DO YOU HAVE TO BE THANKFUL FOR?
THAT'S EASY!
I'M THANKFUL THAT I DON'T HAVE TO WORRY ABOUT "TURKEY DAY"!
11/24-30
©2002 Clint Harmon

HOW'S TH' WORLD BEEN A'TREATIN' YE SLIM?
NOT TOO GOOD DOC!
I ALMOST GOT **ROPED** IN TO A **MARRAGE!**
THET BE UH NASTY **ROPE BURN** YE HAVE THAR SLIM!
DESPERATE LOU!
Email: clintoons@aol.com
©2002 Clint Harmon

JEB, WHEN AIR YE EVER GONNA FIX **TH' FENCE?**
I'LL **IMPLEMENT ACTION** ON THET **RIGHT AWAY!**
HANNIBLE, REMIND ME TO BRING THAT UP AT TH' VERY NEXT **BOARD MEETING!**
?
Email: clintoons@aol.com
©2002 Clint Harmon

MY HOSS NEEDS SHOES! WHAR'S BIG BURLY BOB?
OH, HE RODE OUT TO HOLD UP TH' STAGE!
12/15-21
BIG BURLY BOB
SMITHEY
OH NO! I'LL NEED HELP!
WHUT FER SHERIFF?
©2002 Clint Harmon Email: clintoons@aol.com
BIG BURLY BOB CAN HOLD THAT STAGE UP ALL BY HIMSELF, SO TH' DRIVER CAN REPLACE TH' BROKEN WHEEL!

OOOOOW!
©2002 Clint Harmon
Email: clintoons@aol.com
SORRY HANNIBLE, STANDING ROOM ONLY!
NITE BEFORE XMAS
Happy Holidays
12/22-28

JEB, WE GOT JUST WHAT YOU NEED TO MAKE YOUR LIFE COMPLETE!
Dist.by Clintoons Features
www.rimrockcanyon.com
IT WILL IMPROVE YOUR DEXTERITY, AND HONE YOUR COMPETITIVE SKILLS!
GREAT!
©2003 Clint Harmon Email: clintoons@aol.com
IT BE YER MOVE, HANNIBLE!
?
12/29-1/4

HOWDY DESPERATE LOU! AH SEE TH' SHERIFF HAS YE PUTTIN UP WANTED POSTERS ALL OVER TH' CREATION!
NOPE!
1/5-11
THEY'RE NOT WANTED BAD GUYS POSTERS!
©2003 Clint Harmon Email: clintoons@aol.com
THEY'RE WANTED BACHELOR GUYS POSTERS!
!
OUCH!

SCRUFFY, AH WOULD NEVER LIVE IN NO **ANT HILL** OF A TOWN! LET TH' DESERT **BE MY ABODE** AN' TH' **STARRY SKY** IT'S **ROOF!**
1/12-18
www.rimrockcanyon.com
ROAR! RUMBLE!
©2003 Clint Harmon Email: clintoons@aol.com
YER ROOF JUST SPRUNG A LEAK!

WELCOME TO RIM ROCK EMMA LOU THET BE **GOOD OL' DOC** OVER THAR!
SALOON
JAIL
GENERAL STORE
1/19-25
©2003 Clint Harmon
www.rimrockcanyon.com
HE WILL **NEVER LET YOU DOWN!** BUT I CAN'T SAY TH' SAME FER TH' **OTHER FELLER!**
WHY, JESSIE BELLE?
Email: clintoons@aol.com
HE'S TH' UNDERTAKER!
SALOON
JAIL
GENERAL STORE

1/26-2/1
www.rimrockcanyon.com Dist.By Clintoons Features
AWW COME ON! PLEASE MORTMER! IF'IN AH HAIN'T HOME BY SUPPER TIME, JESSIE BELLE WILL START ANOTHER CIVIL WAR!
©2003 Clint Harmon Email: clintoons@aol.com
SHOOT! MIGHT AS WELL MOSEY ON HOME, TAKES ALL TH' FUN OUT OF IT WHEN THEY POOPS OUT ON YOU!

MIND IF AH SMOKES, MAM?
©2003 Clint Harmon Email: clintoons@aol.com
2/2-8
SWEETIE, LET ME PUT IT THIS WAY, LIGHT THET AN' IT WON'T BE TH' ONLY THING IN HYAR SMOKING!
www.rimrockcanyon.com
HEE HEE; WE BE TH' FIRST STAGE LINE WITH UH DESIGNATED "NO SMOKIN' SECTION"!

LISTEN UP! YOU DUMMY!
www.rimrockcanyon.com
YOU AIM FOR TH' HEART! ...
©2003 Clint Harmon Email: clintoons@aol.com
NOT TH' HAT!
2/9-15

BOY'S! WHAT'ID YE LEARN IN SUNDAY SCHOOL 'BOUT THINGS LIKE THIS?
BOP!
SOK!
WOP!
WELL PARSON, ONE THING COMES TO MIND RIGHT NOW...
... IT'S FAR BETTER TO GIVE THAN TO RECEIVE!
AMEN BROTHER!
©2004 Clint Harmon Email: clintoons@aol.com
3/14-20

OH JEB, I BE SO SAD MY DAFFODIL DIED!
Email: clintoons@aol.com
AN' NOW, MY BEGONIA BE GONE! (SIGH!) OH JEB, WHY CAN'T WE'UNS COME UP WITH ANYTHING....
2/23-3/1
©2003 Clint Harmon
www.rimrockcanyon.com
Dist.By Clintoons Features
THAT'LL LIVE?

BEING A TRAIL DRIVE COOK HAS IT'S UP'S AN' DOWN'S! TAKE TODAY, TH' DOWN SIDE IS TH' BOYS BOYS DIDN'T MUCH CARE FER MA STEW!
MM!
YAK!
GAG!
URP!
Email: clintoons@aol.com
©2003 Clint Harmon
HOWEVER, THE UP SIDE IS...
www.rimrockcanyon.com
... I KNOW NOW WHUT HAPPENED TO THET MISSING BAR O' SOAP!
3/2-8

YIPE! HERE COMES DOUBLE TROUBLE!
I KNOW
©2003 Clint Harmon Email: clintoons@aol.com
...AL AN' CAL TH' BOOMER TWINS!
YE YOUNG'UNS BEHAVE YERSELFS BACK THAR' RIGHT NOW! YA HYAR!
AIR WE THAR YET PA?
3/9-15

PA, MAKE HIM STOP CALLIN' ME AL! AH BE CAL AN' HE BE AL!
www.rimrockcanyon.com
WHOA!
DON'T DRAG ME IN TA THIS! YA BEST SETTLE IT! AS USUAL!
YA HOO!
STOP TH' WAGON PA!
3/16-22
©2003 Clint Harmon Email: clintoons@aol.com
HEH. HEH. BOYS'LL BE BOYS!
BOP!
SOK!
WOP!

WHOA!
©2003 Clint Harmon Email: clintoons@aol.com
www.rimrockcanyon.com
PRAISE BE! AH MADE IT!
WHUT BE TH' PROBLEM? INJUNS?
BANDITS?
~@#%! PRUNES!
3/23-29

GOTCHA! THREE ACES AN' TWO KINGS!
WHOA! HOLD ON THAR!
www.rimrockcanyon.com
3/30-4/5
I'VE GOT FIVE ACES!
©2003 Clint Harmon Email: clintoons@aol.com
WOOPS!
THAT NEW DECK YE CAME UP WITH HAS SURE BROUGHT ME GOOD LUCK!

TIME!
WHEEZE!
4/6-12
©2003 Clint Harmon
Email: clintoons@aol.com
www.rimrockcanyon.com
Dist.By Clintoons Features

WHUT SUBJECT DO YE BOYS LIKE BEST AT SCHOOL?
RITA, 'RITIN' N' 'RITHMETIC!
www.rimrockcanyon.com
Email: clintoons@aol.com
RITA?
©2003 Clint Harmon
SHE BE TH' NEW SCHOOL MARM!
4/13-19

©2003 Clint Harmon
Email: clintoons@aol.com
AH MADE IT! IN TIME FER MY 3 O'CLOCK NAP!
4/20-26

ATTENTION PASSENGERS: PLEASE OBSERVE TH' VIEW ON THE PORT SIDE!
HAIN'T THET A BEAUT OF UH BUTTE?
4/27-5/3
©2003 Clint Harmon Email: clintoons@aol.com

AH! A FRESH POT O' COFFEE, JUST WHAT AH NEEDS FER ME AFTERNOON PICK ME UP!
5/4-10
©2003 Clint Harmon
Email: clintoons@aol.com
WOMAN, YE CALLS THIS COFFEE?
GAG!
NO. AH CALLS IT LYE SOAP WATER AN' VINEGAR! AH BE BOILING OUT TH' COFFEE POT!

WHOA!
A FIVE DOLLAR GOLD PIECE!
©2003 Clint Harmon
WOW! ANOTHER ONE!
AND ANOTHER
WOW! THIS BE MY LUCKY DAY!
WOW! THIS BE MY LUCKY DAY!
Email: clintoons@aol.com
5/11-17

SETH, I WOULD LIKE TO TRY **HYPNOTISM** TO IMPROVE YER **MEMORY!**
IT BE WORTH A SHOT **DOC!**
www.rimrockcanyon.com
WHEN YE AWAKES YOU'LL **REMEMBER** TO **EAT RIGHT**, **EXERCISE**, TAKE YER **PILLS...**
©2003 Clint Harmon Email: clintoons@aol.com
AN' **PAY** YER **DELINQUENT DOCTOR BILLS!**
5/18-24

I DON'T GET IT! HOW CAN YOU STAND A STEADY DIET OF **PUTRID, DISGUSTING,** DEAD **CARCASSES?**
5/25-31
©2003 Clint Harmon
Email: clintoons@aol.com
SIMPLE!
I USE A LOT OF **KETCHUP!**

YAAAAAAAAAAAAAA!!
HEEHAW HEE HAW!
SIGH!
PURRR!
THE WAY YOU'RE SAYING **HOWDY**, ISN'T **WORKING!**
© 2000 Clint Harmon Email: clintoons@aol.com
WHY DON'T YOU JUST **OFFER TO...**
Dist. by Clintoons Features www.rimrockcanyon.com
TO SHAKE HANDS?
YUK! YUK!
6/1-7

IT SAYS HYAR IN TH' **HUBBY HUNTER'S HANDBOOK** THAT "WHAR THAR'S A **WILL** THAR'S A **WAY**"!
DON'T APPEAR **TOO ANXIOUS**, **BE PATIENT!**
6/8-14
©2003 Clint Harmon Email: clintoons@aol.com
PATIENCE POO! WHY WAIT ON THET **WILL FELLER!** AH'LL SETTLE FOR ANY **TOM, DICK** ER **HARRY RIGHT NOW!**

UH OH, LOOKS LIKE PAPPY BOOMER'S TWINS ARE GOING TO FIST CITY AGAIN!
6/15-21
NOT TODAY!
©2003 Clint Harmon Email: clintoons@aol.com
BIG BURLEY BOB'S SUNDAY SCHOOL LESSON FER TODAY IS BROTHERLY LOVE!
SALOON
JAIL
GENRAL STORE

ME AN' OL' HANNIBLE HAVE A MUTUAL AGREEMENT WHEN WE GOES FISHING!
HE DON'T BARK WHILST I HAS A LINE IN TH' WATER! AND I LET'S HIM WANDER AROUND!
6/22-28
©2003 Clint Harmon Email: clintoons@aol.com
GAG! AN ROLL IN DEAD FISH!

HOWDY LUKE! TH' PROBLEM WITH 4TH JULY PICNICS IS ...
©2003 Clint Harmon Email: clintoons@aol.com
... IT TAKES TH' BETTER PART OF UH WEEK TO GET OUR YOUNG'UNS SORTED OUT AGAIN!
6/29–7/5

HOWDY AL AN' CAL! NAMED YER NEW PUPPY YET?
7/6–12
www.rimrockcanyon.com
©2003 Clint Harmon Email: clintoons@aol.com
YEP! HE SUGGESTED IT HIMSELF!
RALPH! RALPH!

OOOOOO!
www.rimrockcanyon.com Dist.By Clintoons Features
STOP HOWLIN' AT TH' MOON HANNIBLE! AN' GET IN HYAR! YE BE KEEPIN' EVERYBODY AWAKE!
7/13-19
©2003 Clint Harmon Email: clintoons@aol.com
ZZZZ
ZZZZ
WORKS EVERY TIME!

LOU, YOU BIG BEAUTIFUL DOLL!
7/20-26
www.rimrockcanyon.com Dist.By Clintoons Features
YE SHOULDN'T BE A'CHASIN' GUYS! THEY SHOULD BE A'CHASIN' YOU!
©2003 Clint Harmon Email: clintoons@aol.com
AH LOVE THIS PLACE!
!?
ECHO VALLEY

TO GET ALONG WITH JESSIE BELLE...
7/27-8/2
©2003 Clint Harmon
APOLOGIZE IF YER WRONG! HOWEVER, IF YUR RIGHT!
Email: clintoons@aol.com
SHUT UP!

OH CUPID, AIM YOUR ARROW STRIGHT N' TRUE! N' SEND ME A TALL, BLOND N' HANDSOME COWBOY WITH EYES O' BLUE!
8/3-9
BUT IF YER GONNA HAVE TO PUT THET ON BACK ORDER...
©2003 Clint Harmon Email: clintoons@aol.com
I'LL TAKE ANYTHING AVAILABLE FER IMMEDIATE DELIVERY!

WHOA NELLIE! "BIG BURLEY BOB" BE DOING HIS WEIGHT LIFTING EXERCISES! ...USING DUMBELLS!
©2003 Clint Harmon Email: clintoons@aol.com
WHAHOO!
YIPEEE!
AN' AL AND CAL BOOMER BE MIGHTY HAPPY TO OBLIGE!
8/10-16

FACE REALITY! FOLKS DON'T LIKE YOU BECAUSE YOU'RE A RATTLE SNAKE AND THEY BITE PEOPLE!
©2003 Clint Harmon Email: clintoons@aol.com
THEY DO!! YAK! GAG! ERK! HOW DISGUSTING!!
www.rimrockcanyon.com Dist.By Clintoons Features
WELL!! WHOSE DUMB IDEA WAS THAT??
8/17-23

ZZZ
8/24-30
POOF!
©2003 Clint Harmon Email: clintoons@aol.com
DON'T YE JUST HATES IT WHEN YE SPENDS ALL NIGHT ON YUR DAYTIME **OCCUPATION!**

PAPPY, PAPPY! WE BE GRADUATIN'
PRAISE BE!
8/31-9/6
YER DEAR **DEPARTED MAW** WOULD BE **SO PROUD!**
©2003 Clint Harmon Email: clintoons@aol.com
TEACHER SAY IF WE PAY ATTENTION, WE MIGHT MAKE IT TO TH' **3RD GRADE!**
OOH!! WHAR DID AH GO **WRONG LUCINDA?**

YOUNG FELLER, WE BE ENTERING VERY DANGEROUS COUNTRY!
INJUNS? BANDITS?
©2003 Clint Harmon Email: clintoons@aol.com
NOPE! NEITHER! MOST CONSIDER THIS TO BE UH FATE WORSE THAN DEATH!!
OH NO! WHAT WILL WE DO?
9/7-13
WHAT'YE MEAN WE? MY AGE SAVES ME FROM DESPERATE LOU'S HUBBY HUNTIN' LASSO!
HI!

DOC. WHAT SHOULD I DO? I KEEP GAINING WEIGHT AN' I'VE TRIED EVERY EXERCISE UNDER TH' SUN...
9/14-20
©2003 Clint Harmon Email: clintoons@aol.com
...I'VE EVEN TRIED PUSH-UPS!
www.rimrockcanyon.com Dist.By Clintoons Features
TRY PUSH-AWAYS!

AL AN' CAL BOOMER, YE BOTH CLAIM TO BE CAL, AN' BLAME EVERYTHING ON YER IDENTICAL TWIN BROTHER! AL! WELL,...
9/21-27
©2003 Clint Harmon
TWO CAN PLAY THIS GAME! O.K. CAL, WHO IS THAT SITTING NEXT TO YE?
AN' IMPOSTOR!
Email: clintoons@aol.com

ANY PROBLEMS SETH ?
ONLY A NAG PROBLEM DOC!
©2003 Clint Harmon
Email: clintoons@aol.com
THAT'S A LITTLE OUT OF MY EXPERTISE, YE NEED A GOOD HORSE DOCTOR!
9/28-10/4
NOW, JUST HOW'S A HOSS DOCTOR GONNA STOP MY WOMAN EMMA LOU'S NAGGING?

SO, YOU'RE A **BIG GAME HUNTER** TOO?
TRUE!
WHAT KIND OF GAME, **BEAR. BUFFALO. MOUNTAIN LION?**
©2003 Clint Harmon Email: clintoons@aol.com
DEALER'S CHOICE!

ON OUR TRIBE'S LAST HUNTING MARITHON I **BAGGED** TH' MOST **BIG BULL BUFFALO!**
www.rimrockcanyon.com
AND OUR TRIBAL HUNTING COUNCIL **VOTED ME AS ...**
WHOA! DON'T TELL ME!
©2003 Clint Harmon Email: clintoons@aol.com
YOU WERE VOTED "**BULL SHOOTER OF TH' YEAR**"!

YES JEB, TH' DOG'S TRULY MAN'S BEST FRIEND!
YE BE RIGHT PARSON!
©2003 Clint Harmon Email: clintoons@aol.com
ZZZ!
HMMM!
WAKE UP! HOW ABOUT A BONE AN' A BELLY RUB FER YER BEST FRIEND!

DESPERATE LOU, I SEE A MAN IN YOUR LIFE IN TH' VERY NEAR FUTURE!
PRAISE BE!
©2003 Clint Harmon Email: clintoons@aol.com
TELL ME. WILL HE BE TALL, BLOND AND HANSOME?
NO! SHORT, BALD, AN' ULGY! HE WILL BE TH' SHERIFF WITH A COURT ORDER TO REPOSSESS YOUR HORSE!

THET BLAMED SHERIFF AN' HIS BLAMED WANTED POSTER!!
?
11/2-8
www.rimrockcanyon.com Dist.By
YE MUST BE UPSET 'CAUSE HES OFFERIN A BIG REWARD FER YOU DEAD ER ALIVE?
©2003 Clint Harmon Email: clintoons@aol.com
NO! BECAUSE HE DIDN'T USE TH' PICTURE OF ME THAT I SENT HIM FER TH' POSTER!

DID YOU EVER THINK ABOUT THE BIG PICTURE, I MEAN WHERE WE COME FROM WHY WE'RE HERE AND WHERE WE'RE GOING?
I KNOW TH' ANSWER TO BOTH QUESTIONS!
11/9-15
YOU DO?
SURE!
©2003 Clint Harmon Email: clintoons@aol.com
I CAME FROM THAT HOLE OVER THERE UNDER THAT ROCK, AN' IF IT GETS ANY HOTTER, THAT'S WHERE I'M GOING!

PAPPY, TEACHER SAY IT'S HIGH TIME YE TOLD US ABOUT TH' BIRDS AN' BEES!
11/16-22 Dist.By Clintoons Features
©2003 Clint Harmon Email: clintoons@aol.com
FORGIVE ME BOYS. I'M SORRY TO LET YE DOWN, BUT...
YER DEAR DEPARTED GRANDPAPPY FORGOT TO TELL ME!
www.rimrockcanyon.com

SOUNDS LIKE FOLKS ARE OUT EXTENDING INVITATIONS TO THANKSGIVING DINNER!
11/23-29
SIGH! NOBODY EVER INVITES ME TO THANKSGIVING DINNER!
©2003 Clint Harmon Email: clintoons@aol.com
I'LL BET THAT WILD TURKEY WISHES HE COULD SAY TH' SAME!
ZING!
ZING!
ZING!

TO READ THE SECOND FEATURE

Next of Kin

GO TO BACK COVER AND READ FORWARD ▸▸

WHAT YOU KIDS NEED AROUND HERE IS A **CUTE, CUDDLY** LITTLE SOMETHING TO LOVE!
RIGHT DAD. AND WE'VE TAKEN CARE OF **THAT!**
ALL RIGHT!
CONTINUED...
MEET **"JOSE"** WE GOT HIM AT TH' **PET SHOP** IN TH' **MALL!**
EEEK!
WHAT IS IT?
WELL, MOM ALWAYS THOUGHT I WAS **KINDA CUTE!**

UNCLE OBIE, I'M AFRAID I CAN'T MAKE OUR CHESS GAME THIS EVENING
CAN'T MAKE IT? JUST **REMEMBER...**
...WHERE THERE'S A **WILL**, THERE'S A **WAY!**
SAME TIME?
GOOD BOY!

THAT'S WHY I DON'T LIKE ALL **YOU CAN EAT BUFFETS**, YOU DON'T HAVE A CLUE AS TO WHEN YOU'VE HAD **ALL YOU CAN EAT!**
NOT SO!! THAT'S EASY TO TELL!
IT'S WHEN THEY START RUNNING LOW ON TH' **GOOD STUFF!**

?
???
WHERE DE FUNNIES?
THIS MUST BE WHY IT'S CALLED A "DOG'S LIFE" THERE'S NOBODY LEFT TO TAKE IT OUT ON!
OH, I DON'T KNOW GRRRR! HOW 'BOUT FLEAS?
YIPE! WHAT'S EATIN' HIM?
US, STUPID!

SO HOW'S MARRIED LIFE AFTER THE FIRST YEAR DEB?
I LOVE KEN VERY MUCH, BUT I'VE HAD TO DEAL WITH HIS OTHER LOVES!
OH NO! YOU POOR DEAR!
YEAH, HOW DO YOU COMPETE WITH A PEPPERONI PIZZA?

NO, NO, NO, DEB, YOU'RE DOING IT ALL WRONG!
YOU'LL WASH TH' PLANTS RIGHT OUT OF TH' GROUND! HOLD IT UP! HOLD IT UP!
TOO HIGH!

I LOST ME FRONT YARD PRIVILEGES FOR BECOMING TOO **ATTACHED TO TH' MAIL MAN!**
ON MY WALKS ALL **FIRE PLUGS** HAVE BEEN DECLARED **"OFF LIMITS"**!
IT'S THAT DARN CAT. SOMEBODY ALWAYS HAS IT IN THEIR LAP **STROKING ITS EARS!**
GROUP THERAPY!

YOU EATING AGAIN?
IS IT OK TO MAKE A SANDWICH OUT OF THAT STUFF IN TH' LITTLE GREEN PLASTIC CONTAINER IN THE FRIDGE?
WELL, IT'S OK WITH ME...
IF IT'S OK WITH **JOSE!**

OH BOY! MY FAVORITE MAGAZINE!
I JUST CAN'T WAIT TO TAKE A PEEK AT THIS MONTH'S CENTERFOLD!
WOW! WHAT A DISH!
PRIME RIB SURROUNDED BY LITTLE NEW POTATOES WITH PARSLEY AND BUTTERED BABY CARROTS!
FOOD REVIEW

EVERYBODY OUR AGE ALREADY HAS GRANDCHILDREN! IT'S JUST NOT FAIR!
WELL, IT'S SURE NOT MY FAULT!
HMM.... NOW THAT YOU MENTION IT!.... I WONDER...
.... DID YOU REALLY EVER HAVE THOSE LITTLE FATHER AND SON TALKS WITH KENNY?

ALL RIGHT, LUNCH!
WE'RE FORTUNATE TO BE COMPUTER'S!
HOW SO?
THEIR MEMORY FADES WITH EACH PASSING YEAR WHILE OURS IS ENHANCED WITH EACH PROGRAM UPDATE! YES, WE DEFINITELY HAVE THE EDGE ON EM!
EXCEPT FOR ONE THING!
WE CAN'T CALL IN SICK!

WAKE UP KENNY! TH' LIGHT IS GREEN!
HOW COME THEY'RE NOT HONKING AT YOU AS USUAL?
YOU HAVEN'T NOTICED MY NEW BUMPER STICKER!
HONK IF YOU LIKE MY DRIVING

JUST A LITTLE GIFT THAT WE HOPE WILL BE USEFUL IN THE VERY **NEAR FUTURE!**
GEE THANKS DAD!
PRE-NATAL CARE

GURGLE! GRRRR!
?
ITS NOON! TH' CLOCK IS **SLOW!**
HOW WOULD YOU KNOW? YOU DON'T HAVE A WATCH! ...BUT BY GOLLY **YOU'RE RIGHT!**
SOME SOURCES OF INFORMATION ARE FAR MORE ACCURATE THAN ***MERE TIME PIECES!***

THE BAD PART ABOUT BEING AS OLD AS I AM IS THAT ALL YOUR OLD FRIENDS ARE GONE!
HOWEVER!
SO ARE ALL YOUR OLD ENEMIES!

HOW COME UNCLE OBIE NEVER MARRIED?
HE COULDN'T BE UNFAITHFUL TO HIS FIRST LOVE!
ALONE AT LAST, WE SHOULD SPEND MORE QUALITY TIME LIKE THIS TOGETHER!

FIVE O'CLOCK AROUND HERE LOOKS LIKE A TRAIL DRIVE **STAMPEDE!**
NOW THAT'S DEDICATION FOR YOU, STICKING TO HIS WORK STATION TILL' TH' LAST PROBLEM OF TH' DAY IS **SOLVED!**
PROBLEM HAH! HE WAS WATCHING TH' ANIMATED SCREEN SAVER AN HE MUST OF **DOZED OFF!**

I JUST GOT HOME AND IT'S TOO LATE TO FIX DINNER. HOW ABOUT ORDERING A ***PIZZA?***
GURGLE PURRRR!
FINE, PEPPERONI WITH DOUBLE CHEESE, ***RIGHT!***
UNIVERSAL LANGUAGE!

WHAT MAKES YOU THINK TH' NEW GUY IS COMPUTER **ILLITERATE?**
HE THINKS A **MEGABYTE** IS A HUGE **BLOODSUCKIN' PARASITE!**
HA HA HA HA HA HA HO HO
HO HO HO HA HA HA HA HA HA HA HA
VERY FUNNY! HIS FIRST WEEK HERE HE THOUGHT A **"HARD DRIVE"** WAS A NON-STOP TRIP TO **PHOENIX!**

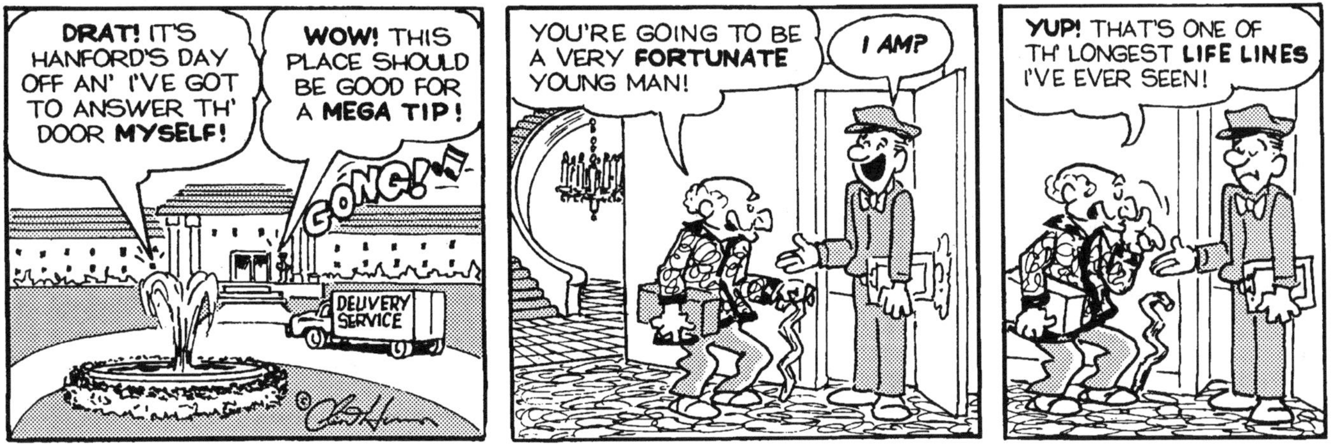
DRAT! IT'S HANFORD'S DAY OFF AN' I'VE GOT TO ANSWER TH' DOOR **MYSELF!**
WOW! THIS PLACE SHOULD BE GOOD FOR A **MEGA TIP!**
GONG!
DELIVERY SERVICE
YOU'RE GOING TO BE A VERY **FORTUNATE** YOUNG MAN!
I AM?
YUP! THAT'S ONE OF TH' LONGEST **LIFE LINES** I'VE EVER SEEN!

IF I WASN'T ON A LEASH I'D HAVE YOU FOR BREAKFAST RUNT!
GRRR!
OH YEAH, I BET MY FLEAS CAN WHIP YOURS!
YAP! YAPPITY, YAP!
SORRY, AIN'T NOBODY HERE BUT US CHICKENS!
CLUCK! CLUCK! CLUCK! CLUCK! CLUCK! CLUCK! CLUCK! CLUCK

HI HOWARD! WHAT DO YOU THINK OF MY NEW DOG!
THAT'S A DOG?
I THOUGHT IT WAS A MOUSE WITH A GLAND PROBLEM!

SINCE I HAVE BEEN ON THIS DIET I FEEL UNCONTROLLABLY DRAWN TO FOOD LIKE METALTO A MAGNET!
Elite RESTAURANT
SAY WAITER, COULD WE PLEASE HAVE ANOTHER TABLE... ONE NOT SO CLOSE TO THE WINDOW?

KENNY, WHEN I WAS A YOUNG MAN NONE OF THEM PRETTY YOUNG THINGS WOULD GIVE ME A SECOND LOOK!
HEH, HEH, BUT NOW I WOULDN'T GIVE THEM A SECOND LOOK!
CHUCKLE! TOO OLD EH UNCLE OBIE?
SHUCKS NO! THEM'S ALL OLD LADIES NOW!

IT'S ALWAYS **HER DOG** WHEN SHE SHOWS HIM OFF!
OF COURSE AT TIMES HE'S ***MY DOG*** TOO!
LIKE WHEN HE ***MISSES TH' PAPER!***

HEY DEB! LET JOSE IN!
RING!
YOUR DOG RINGS THE **DOORBELL??**
HAH HAH! NO DAD, HE CAN'T RING TH' **DOORBELL!**
...HE RECRUITS HELP!

WHINE! WHIMPER!
NOT NOW!
AFTERWHILE!
HE **TALKS** TH' **TALK** BUT HE DON'T **WALK** TH' **WALK!**

WHOA! $500.00 CREDIT CARD CHARGE??
DEB!
LOOK AT THAT! WHAT IS THAT? DO YOU MIND TELLING ME **WHAT THAT IS? ??**
HMMM!
IT'S YOUR **LEFT FOREFINGER. SILLY!**

WOW, WITH MY NEW SATELLITE DISH THERE'S SO MANY GREAT EDUCATIONAL PROGRAMS ON TV. . .
. . . I CAN'T DECIDE WHAT TO WATCH! ENIEE, MEENIE, MINEY . . .
CLICK! CLICK! CLICK!
. . . MOE, CURLY AND LARRY!
BOP! SLAP! POKE! YUK! YUK!
CLICK!

HELLO HANFORD, IS MY UNCLE OBIE THERE?
I BELIEVE NURSE SHAPELY IS GIVING HIM HIS DAILY EXERCISES IN THE GARDEN, SIR.

YOU'LL BE HAPPY HERE "PRINCESS"! LOOK! WE HAVE A LITTLE FRIEND TO KEEP YOU COMPANY!
!
!
?
?
IF IT'S ALL THE SAME TO YOU I'D RATHER HAVE A BALL OF YARN!!

I'M TH' SECURITY HERE! I PROTECT THIS FAMILY!
WHAT GOOD ARE YOU AROUND HERE ANYWAY?
HEY! BEING CUTE IS A FULL TIME JOB!

GOOD DOG!
?
...I GET IT NOW! THAT'S ONE OF THOSE...
MECHANICAL DOGS. PAT IT ON THE HEAD AND IT SLOBBERS ALL OVER YOU!

SOMEBODY HAS BEEN EATING MY FOOD!
SOMEBODY HAS BEEN DRINKING MY WATER!
SOMEBODY HAS BEEN SLEEPING IN MY PLACE!
... AND SHE IS STILL THERE!
PRRRR! PRRR!

HEY DEB!
CALL AND SEE WHAT HAPPENED TO OUR PIZZA DELIVERY! ...
MY STOMACH IS GROWLING LIKE CRAZY!
GRRRRRRR! GROWLLL!

SO BUSINESS SUDDENTLY FELL OFF, EH?
©2003 Clint Harmon
I THINK I KNOW WHAT YOUR PROBLEM IS!
10/5 -11
Email: clintoons@aol.com
YE NEED AN ADVERTISING CONSULTANT!
HELD OVER FOR SECOND BIG WEEK! OUR SPECIAL RECIPE CHICKEN NOODLE SOUP!

HON, I'VE GOT GOOD NEWS, I'VE ORDERED A PIZZA WITH ALL YOUR FAVORITE TOPPINGS!
ALRIGHT!
BUT HOLD ON, I'VE ALSO GOT SOME BAD NEWS!
AW LAY IT ON ME, TH' GOOD NEWS WILL HELP ME HANDLE IT!
EAT, DRINK AND BE MERRY, FOR TOMORROW YOU DIET!
IT DIDN'T HELP!

WHOA! A PACKAGE OF FROZEN LIVER THAWING, ALONG WITH SOME ONIONS!
I HATE LIVER 'N ONIONS!
HEY DEB! LET'S EAT OUT TONIGHT!
TH' OL' "THAWING LIVER AN' ONIONS" PLOY NEVER FAILS!

IT'S A NEAT WORLD WE LIVE IN. DON'T YOU THINK?
YUP!
HOWEVER, I DO HAVE A COUPLE COMPLAINTS!
TOO MANY FLEAS, AN' NOT ENOUGH TREES!

WHOA! KING SOLMON HAD 700 WIVES! NOW, YA' JUST GOT'TA HAVE SYMPATHY FOR A GUY LIKE THAT!
HAH! MAY I ASK WHY?
JUST VISUALIZE ALL 700 OF 'EM NAGGING AT ONCE!
NOT TO MENTION TH' MOTHER-IN-LAW PROBLEMS!

MAY I BUTT-IN HERE?
WELL! PARDON ME!
WAIT! I WOULD LIKE TO RE-PHRASE THAT!
... GET YOUR BUTT OUT OF THERE!
NZZZ!

YOU KNOW KEN, BACK WHEN I WAS JUST A NEW POTATO ...
SOME FOLKS THOUGHT I WAS ONE HOT POTATO!
AN' TO PURTY YOUNG THINGS I WAS A SWEET POTATO!
BUT NOW, THEY ALL THINK I'M JUST UH OLD POTATO!

HI THERE! ARE YOU NEW AROUND HERE?
UH OH, GOT'TA GO NOW...
TAKE CARE! AND DON'T BE A STRANGER!
SIGH!! THAT WAS A CLOSE ONE!

SNORE!
ZZZ
I THINK I KNOW WHY HE LIKES TO WATCH OLD RERUNS! IF HE NODS OFF...
POOF!
AND THEN WAKES UP SUDDENTLY!
HEE! HEE! HAWHAW!
HE HASN'T MISSED A THING!
©2003 Clint Harmon Email: clintoons@aol.com 9/28- 10/4
www.rimrockcanyon.com Dist.By Clintoons Features

IS THAT SO? I'M SURE THAT YOU ARE AWARE THAT MAN WAS CREATED FIRST!... SO WE GOT SENIORITY ON YA! HEH. HEH!
OK.OK. SO MAN WAS FIRST! BUT. I'M SO GLAD THAT ...
...WE HAVE THE NEW AND IMPROVED VERSION!

OOOH! ME! MAYBE A NICE. GORY HORROR MOVIE WILL GET MY MIND OFF MY DIET!
CLICK!
OOH NO!!! I CAN'T TAKE THIS!!
ON A SESAME SEED BUN!
COMMERCIAL BREAK!!
SIP!

WHOA! THIS LOOKS LIKE TH' NATIONAL DEBT!
YOU KNOW DEB. WE SHOULD OF LIVED B.C.!
B.C.??
YEAH. BEFORE CREDIT CARDS. WHEN YOU COULD SEE. FEEL AND FONDLE YOUR MONEY BEFORE YOU SPENT IT!

WELL SON, WE DID IT! WE JOINED TH' S.C.D.G.!
WHAT'S THAT DAD. YOUR NEW HMO?
?
NO. IT'S A SUPPORT GROUP FOR...
SENIOR CITIZENS DEPRIVED OF GRANDCHILDREN!

HOLD THAT THOUGHT! I'LL BE RIGHT BACK!
!
WOW. WAS I EVER THIRSTY!
WHOA! WHAT'S THIS?
I'M SORRY MA'AM, BUT THIS SEAT IS TAKEN!

HEY! THAT'S NOT FAIR!
SMOOCH!
IT'S TIME FOR MY LAP NAP!
OH WELL! IF YOU CAN'T BEAT'EM JOIN 'EM!
ZIP!

AS HIS ANCESTORS DID IN THE WILD. THE BRAVE AND NOBLE DOG ...
GRRRRR!
...KEEPS EVIL POACHERS AWAY FROM HIS **PRIVATE TERRITORY!**
GRRRR!
LAPLAND! GRRRRR!

HERE' YOUR LI'L **RED** PILL...
YOUR LI'L **BLUE** PILL...
ORANGE PILL!
GREEN PILL!
AND **YELLOW** PILL!
WHO SAYS LIFE AFTER **90** CAN'T **BE COLORFUL?**

DO YOU REALIZE, YOU'VE BEEN WEARING THAT VERY SAME TIE FOR A SOLID WEEK?
HUH?
REALLY? NOW, THAT'S A RECORD BREAKER!
WHAT? YOU'RE PROUD OF THAT?
YOU BET! TWO WEEKS AND STILL NO GRAVY!

PHEW! TH' TRAFFIC OUT THERE IS UNREAL!
GRRR!
ZZ
EEEEYOW!
OOH! POOR BABY I'M SO SORRY!
WHINE! THAT'S OK. TH' GAIN'S WORTH TH' PAIN!
OW! TH' DARN CAT HARPOONED ME WITH 'ER CLAWS!

SNIFF!
SNIFF!
WHINE!
SNIFF!
HONK!
HONK!
SNIFF!
SNIFF!
SNIFF SNIFF!
IT HAPPENS EVERY TIME WE WATCH OL' YELLER!
WHINE!
SNIFF!
SNIFF!

HELLO HANFORD! IS UNCLE OBIE THERE?
HE'S AT THE THE PLAZA WITH NURSE SHAPELY!
HEY BIMBO! WE GOT TH' RIGHT O' WAY HERE!
LOOK WHERE YOUR GOING YOU DIP!
MOVE IT! ROAD-BLOCK!
YOU THERE, WITH ALL TH' COUPONS, MY POTATOS ARE BEGINNING TO SPROUT!
SHOPPING CART RAGE!
CHECK OUT

CAREFUL WITH YOUR TIE DEAR!
HEY! CHECK IT OUT! TWO WEEKS AND STILL NO GRAVY!
UH OH!
DOES TARTAR SAUCE COUNT?

HMM! I DON'T KNOW QUITE HOW TO TELL YOU THIS DEAR. ...BUT THIS STEW ISN'T UP TO YOUR USUAL STANDARDS!
?
WELL. THANK YOU DEAR! EXCUSE ME A MINUTE...
...TH' CAN LABEL SAYS TO CALL THIS 800 NUMBER WITH YOUR COMMENTS!

WE PICKED UP A LITTLE SOMETHING HERE AT TH' MALL FOR YOU TO TAKE HOME WITH YOU KENNY!
A TEDDY BEAR FOR ME, DAD?
?
OH NO, THAT'S FOR LITTLE YOU KNOW **WHO WHENEVER**!
DAD!
WELL, IT HAS **BEEN TEN MONTHS**!
?
?
?
?
?

HA HA HA HA HA HA HA HA
HAHA HA HA HA HA HA
HEY CLYDE, LOOK AT THIS!
?
HA HA HA HA HA HA HA
HO HO HA HA HA HA HAHA
ACTUALLY, I DIDN'T GET IT... BUT YOU CAN'T HAVE FOLKS THINKING YOU'RE **VOID OF A SENSE OF HUMOR**!
HEH! HEH!

AFTER ALL THESE YEARS I FINALLY HAVE ENOUGH **MONEY** TO DO WHAT I'VE **ALWAYS WANTED!**
THATS GREAT UNCLE OBIE!
NOT REALLY!
I'VE FORGOT NOW WHAT IT WAS THAT I ALWAYS **WANTED TO DO!**

OKAY, I CAN UNDERSTAND CHASING AN OCCASIONAL CAR...
BUT THIS IS **RIDICULOUS!**
BIKE TRAIL

HAH! HE DOESN'T EVEN KNOW WHY YOU SPREAD THOSE PAPERS!
HEY! I DO TOO!
IT MUST BE SO I CAN FOLLOW MY COMIC STRIP HERO **"BERT TH' DOG"!**

HON. JUST HOW OLD IS YOUR **GREAT UNCLE OBIE?**
WOW! I DON'T THINK ANYONE KNOWS FOR SURE!
I WONDER WHAT'S HIS SECRET FOR **LONGEVITY?**
HMMM! THERE'S A FAMILY RUMOR ...
... THAT WHEN HE FOUND OUT HE COULDN'T TAKE IT WITH HIM. ***HE DECIDED NOT TO GO!***

LETS GET THIS STRAIGHT JOSE! YOU SEE THIS FOOD? THIS IS MY FOOD! GOT THAT?
YAP!
YAP!
YUP!
YOU SEE TH' FOOD IN THAT DISH? THAT'S YOUR FOOD! GOT THAT?
YAP!
YAP!
YUP!
TRADE JA!

SIGH! WE DIDN'T GET A PAPER TODAY!
YEAH! I SURE MISSED TH' PAPER TODAY!
HAH! SEE I'M NOT TH' ONLY ONE!

FEELING POOPED EH, UNCLE OBIE? HAVE YOU BEEN GETTING ENOUGH SLEEP?
NOT REALLY!
I WAS UP ALL NIGHT WITH THE GHOSTS OF **XMAS PAST, PRESENT** AND **FUTURE!**

?!
RATTLE
THANKS FOLKS! BUT, I DON'T THINK THIS WILL FIT ME!
2002
OH, WE LIKE TO GIVE GIFTS THAT PROVIDE AN **INCENTIVE** FOR THE NEW YEAR!

WOW! THIS IS GREAT! WHAT'S IN IT DEB?
I'LL CHECK TH' LABEL!
SOY LECETHIN, CHICKEN FAT, MONOSODIUM GLUTIMATE, DEHYDRATED VEGETABLES, ARTIFICIAL FLAVOR AND COLOR, ETC, ETC!
SIGH! NO WONDER ADAM AND EVE WERE A LOT HAPPIER BEFORE ATTAINING ALL THAT KNOWLEDGE!

I'M SURE THIS DOG FOOD PROVIDES ALL TH' ESSENTIAL NUTRITION A DOG NEEDS FOR HEALTHY BONES, MUSCLES, AND A SHINY COAT!
HOWEVER ...
I STILL SAY THAT THEY'VE GOT ALL TH' GOOD STUFF IN THERE!

YOU KNOW IT'S THE **10TH DAY** OF YOUR DIET ...
WHEN YOUR **STOMACH...**
STARTS SENDING YOU **HOSTILE MESSAGES!**
GRRRR! GROWL! GURGLE! #!!☆M!!
GRRR!

DID YOU HAVE ANYTHING ELSE FOR LUNCH EXCEPT THAT **DIET SANDWICH** I MADE FOR YOU?
NOPE! THAT WAS ALL I HAD AT **NOON!**
OH! I'M **SOOO PROUD** OF YOU!
HEY! AREN'T YOU GOING TO TELL HER ABOUT THAT **CHEESEBURGER** AN' **MALT** AT **3'OCLOCK BREAK?**

WOW! IT'S GETTING HOT IN HERE! SOMEBODY OUGHTTO ADJUST TH' THERMOSTAT!
HAPPY BIRTHDAY UNCLE OBIE
WHEEZE!
POOF!
EITHER THAT, OR HELP UNCLE OBIE BLOW OUT THOSE CANDLES!

HEY! THIS SOUP TASTES FUNNY!
GEE! I'M SORRY!
AND I WANT YOU TO KNOW THAT I WOULD FIRE THE COOK RESPONSABLE FOR THAT SOUP BUT...
POOF!
HE QUIT TWO WEEKS AGO!

WOW! IT'S SO COOL TH' WAY THESE COMIC STRIP DOGS WALK AROUND ON TWO LEGS! I'LL BET I COULD DO THAT!
HEY! IF I GET REALLY GOOD AT IT. MAYBE THEY'LL LET ME SET AT TH' TABLE!
TO BE CONTINUED

HEY, IF "BERT TH' DOG" IN TH' COMIC STRIP CAN WALK AROUND ON TWO LEGS. I CAN TOO! IT SHOULD MAKE ME TOP DOG AROUND HERE!
HAH! THIS IS A PIECE OF CAKE! READY TO RUMBLE!
?
?
HAH! THEY'RE NOTICING! EAT YOUR HEART OUT CAT!

I'M DOING IT! I'M DOING IT! I'M WALKIN' ON TWO LEGS JUST LIKE TH' COMIC STRIP DOGS!
?
OOOOOW!
SNAP!
CRACK
POP!
I THINK I SLIPPED UH DISC!
ALL I GOT TO SHOW FOR TRYING TO WALK ON TWO LEGS LIKE TH' COMIC STRIP DOGS, IS AN ACHING BACK!
I GUESS THAT IF THE GOOD LORD HAD MEANT FOR ME TO WALK ON TWO LEGS...
I WOULDN'T HAVE BEEN OUTFITTED WITH FOUR!

I KNOW THAT THIS ISN'T YOUR REGULAR DOG FOOD BUT, IT LOOKS **DELICIOUS!**
SNIFF!
MMMM! SMELLS GOOD TOO! I BET IT DOESN'T TASTE **HALF** BAD!
OK, I'M SOLD. BUT, ONLY IF YOU GET **HALF!** AN' YOU ...
EAT YOUR HALF FIRST!
©2002 Clint Harmon Dist.by Clintoons Features
Email: clintoons@aol.com
www.rimrockcanyon.com
3/10-16

I'LL BET YOU'RE REALLY ENJOYING RETIREMENT ***"DOING JUST AS YOU PLEASE"! RIGHT DAD?***
NOT EXACTLY...
I AM ***" DOING JUST AS SHE PLEASES"!***
©2002 Clint Harmon
Dist.by Clintoons Features
3/17-23
Email: clintoons@aol.com
www.rimrockcanyon.com

GEE, IT'S GREAT OF YOU TO TAKE ME OUT TO LUNCH UNCLE OBIE!
HEY, YOU'RE MY FAVORITE GREAT NEPHEW!
©2002 Clint Harmon Dist.by Clintoons Features
I'M YOUR ONLY GREAT NEPHEW!
WHATEVER! NOTHING IS TOO GOOD FOR FAMILY!
Email: clintoons@aol.com
www.rimrockcanyon.com
TWO MINI BURGERS USING COUPONS AND WITH SENIOR DISCOUNT!
ORDER
DRIVE THRU
3/24-30

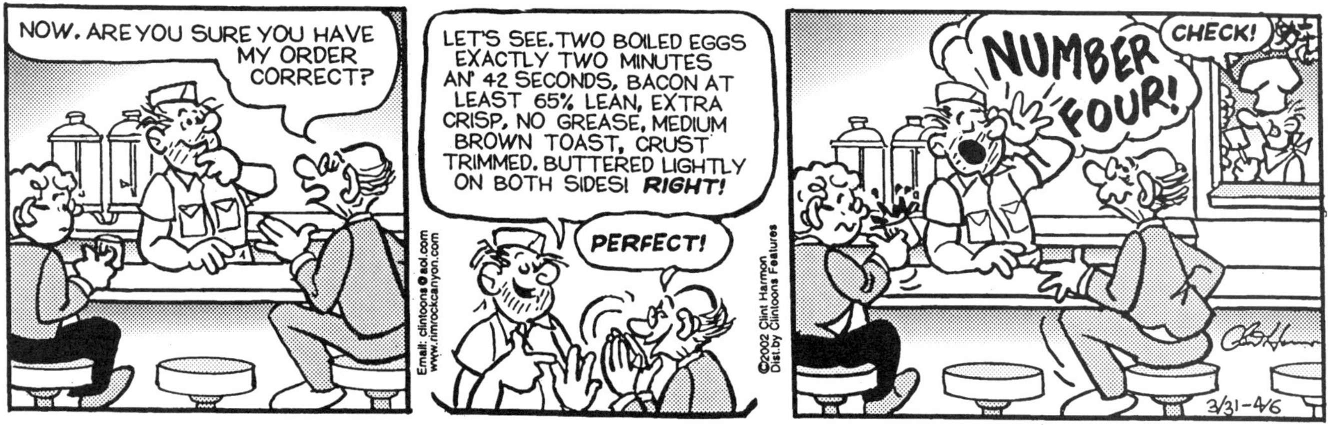
NOW. ARE YOU SURE YOU HAVE MY ORDER CORRECT?
Email: clintoons@aol.com
www.rimrockcanyon.com
LET'S SEE. TWO BOILED EGGS EXACTLY TWO MINUTES AN' 42 SECONDS, BACON AT LEAST 65% LEAN, EXTRA CRISP, NO GREASE, MEDIUM BROWN TOAST, CRUST TRIMMED. BUTTERED LIGHTLY ON BOTH SIDES! RIGHT!
PERFECT!
©2002 Clint Harmon Dist.by Clintoons Features
NUMBER FOUR!
CHECK!
3/31-4/6

YOU KNOW IT'S TH' **FIRST WEEK** OF YOUR **DIET WHEN...**
Email: clintoons@aol.com Dist.by Clintoons Features
THE ONLY "**GOOD OL' DAYS**" YOU CAN REMEMBER IS...
4/7-13
LAST THURSDAY NIGHT'S ***PIZZA!***
©2002 Clint Harmon

OH NO!
WHINE!
4/14-20
NOW THAT'S AN EXAMPLE OF WHY I SAY THERE'S ***TOO MUCH VIOLENCE*** ON TV!
©2002 Clint Harmon
BOY, TH' KITTY ALMOST GOT TH' TWITTY THAT TIME!
BAD, BAD PUTTY TAT!
Email: clintoons@aol.com

YOUR WILL LOOKS IN GOOD ORDER, DO YOU HAVE A BURIAL POLICY?
NOPE!
4/21-27
©2002 Clint Harmon Dist.by Clintoons Features
I NEVER WORRY ABOUT THINGS IN ADVANCE!
Email: clintoons@aol.com
I'LL JUST WAIT AND GET THREE ESTIMATES!

IT'S GREAT TO HAVE MY VERY OWN...
©2002 Clint Harmon
Dist.by Clintoons Features
CHEF,
...MAID.
VALET!
4/28-5/4
Email: clintoons@aol.com
I GUESS YOU COULD SAY I'M LIVING IN THE LAP OF LUXURY!

QUIT COMPLAINING! IT'S AN UNWRITTEN LAW THAT HUSBANDS MUST DO AT LEAST 60% OF THE HOUSEHOLD CHORES!
5/5-11
OH YEAH! PROVE IT!
I CAN'T DO THAT SILLY! IT HASN'T BEEN WRITTEN YET!
Email: clintoons@aol.com
©2002 Clint Harmon

FASTER. FASTER JOSE!
WHY? ARE WE CHASING SOMEONE OR IS SOMEONE CHASING US?
WHOA!
PIT STOP!
5/12-18
Email: clintoons@aol.com
©2002 Clint Harmon Dist.by Clintoons Features

WELL, I MUST SAY YOU ARE IMPROVING, THE PIZZA IS LUKEWARM THIS TIME!
5/19-25
©2002 Clint Harmon
YOUNG MAN WOULD YOU LIKE FOR ME TO GIVE YOU A VALUABLE TIP?
YOU BET!
TO AVOID LIFE'S DISAPPOINMENTS, MAINTAIN A LOW EXPECTATION LEVEL!
Email: clintoons@aol.com

LOOK! DOESN'T MS.JONES LOOK GREAT AFTER HER "FACE LIFT"?
5/26-6/1
Email: clintoons@aol.com
WHOA! ARE YOU SURE THAT'S LEGAL?
POSTIVE! WHY?
©2002 Clint Harmon Dist.by Clintoons Features
WELL, TURNING BACK THE SPEEDOMETER ON YOU CAR ISN'T!

SO, YOU'RE EXPECTING A GRANDCHILD, I'LL BET YOU ARE **THRILLED**
NOT REALLY!
©2002 Clint Harmon
Email: clintoons@aol.com
YOU SEE WE HAVE BEEN EXPECTING A GRANDCHILD FOR SOME TIME NOW...
BUT, WE CAN'T SEEM TO GET ANY **COOPERATION!**
6/2-8

6/9-15
"YELL-A-PHONE" FOR YOU SIR!
©2002 Clint Harmon
YOU **RAISED** MY **LEASE OPTION** YOU **PENNYPINCHING**, CONIVING, **MONEY**...
GRUBBING OLD **SCROUNDLE.** YOU HAVEN'T CHANGED A BIT IN 40 YEARS!
Email: clintoons@aol.com
IF IT AIN'T **BROKE** DON'T **FIX IT!**

SMACK!
WOW! WHAT WAS THAT FOR?
Dist.by Clintoons Features Email: clintoons@aol.com
6/6-22
FOR NOTHING TEE HEE!
BUT I DIDN'T "DO NOTHING" SO I DON'T DESERVE IT!
Email: clintoons@aol.com
SO THE ONLY HONEST THING TO DO IS GIVE IT BACK TO YOU!
SMOOCH!

WHOA! THEY HAVE SLIPPED SOME OF THAT DRY STUFF IN ON ME!
6/23-29
Email: clintoons@aol.com
THANK YOU LORD FOR WHAT WE ARE ABOUT TO RECEIVE!
?
©2002 Clint Harmon
SPEAK FOR YOURSELF!

WE WANT ONE WITHOUT THE **HARD DRIVE!**
?
YOU WANT A **COMPUTER** WITHOUT A ***HARD DRIVE?***
6/30-7/6
Email: clintoons@aol.com
MY YES, I'LL BE NEW ON THE CYBER SPACE SUPER HIGHWAY, AND I WANT AN ***EASY DRIVE!***
©2002 Clint Harmon

WITH **E-MAIL WE CAN** KEEP IN TOUCH WITH TH' **KIDS! AND** PERHAPS PERSUADE THEM TO...
7/1-13
©2002 Clint Harmon
Dist.by Clintoons Features Email: clintoons@aol.com
PROVIDE US WITH ***LITTLE THINGS*** TO MAKE OUR GOLDEN YEARS ***HAPPIER!***
LITTLE THINGS LIKE ***"GRANDCHILDREN"!***

YOU GOT MAIL!
!
AHH HAH!
SO. THAT'S WHERE TH' MAILMAN HAS BEEN HOLED UP THESE LAST FEW DAYS!
7/14-20
©2002 Clint Harmon
Email: clintoons@aol.com

AARRGG!
?
I KNEW THIS WOULD HAPPPEN IF MOM GOT A COMPUTER! JUST LISTEN TO THIS E-MAIL...
ROSES ARE RED, VIOLETS ARE BLUE, IF WE CAN'T HAVE A GRANDDAUGHTER, A GRANDSON WILL DO! LOVE, WANNABE GRANNIE.COM
1/21-27
©2002 Clint Harmon
Dist.by Clintoons Features Email: clintoons@aol.com

MAN. I LOVE THIS TIME OF TH' YEAR. WITH TH' BIRDS CHIRPIN' AN' TH' BEES BUZZIN'!
I THINK EVERYBODY OUGHT TO TAKE TH' TIME TO SMELL TH'...
...TREES!
©2002 Clint Harmon
Email: clintoons@aol.com
7/28-8/3

OH NO, I FORGOT MY BILLFOLD!
I'LL MAKE AN EXCEPTION THIS TIME, EAT NOW, PAY LATER!
EXCEPTION! HAH!
ANYBODY THAT HAS EVER EATEN HERE PAID LATER!
8/4-10
©2002 Clint Harmon Email: clintoons@aol.com

I'LL NEVER FORGET THE DAY DAD LET ME DRIVE FOR THE **FIRST TIME!**
I'LL BET IT WAS **THRILL...**
8/11-17
...TO DRIVE A CAR FOR THE FIRST **TIME!**
CAR!! WHAT CAR?
IT WAS A SPANKIN' NEW RUBBER TIRED BUGGY WITH **GENUINE HORSEPOWER!**
©2002 Clint Harmon Email: clintoons@aol.com

NOW, WHAT DID I DO?
LEMONS
IT'S NOT WHAT YOU **DID,** IT'S WHAT YOU **SAID!**
8/18-24
©2002 Clint Harmon Email: clintoons@aol.com
HEY! ALL I SAID WAS "**I AM GOOD AT PICKING LEMONS**"!
LEM

DID YOU REMEMBER WHAT TODAY IS?
OF COURSE!
8/25 -31
©2002 Clint Harmon
I WOULDN'T FORGET AN IMPORTANT THING LIKE THAT!
SIGH! HE DID REMEMBER OUR 40TH WEDDING ANNIVERSARY!
Email: clintoons@aol.com
IT'S THURSDAY AUGUST THE 29TH. MY DENTAL APPOINTMENT!
CONTINUED NEXT WEEK.
Clint Harmon

HAPPY ANNIVERSARY MOM AN' DAD!
YES, WE'VE BEEN HAPPILY MARRIED FOR 40 YEARS!
©2002 Clint Harmon
HOWEVER...
Email: clintoons@aol.com
THIS MORNING I WOULD HAVE TRADED HIM FOR AN OLD BREAD WRAPPER!
Clint Harmon 9/1-7

FIRST IT WAS THAT CAT!
9/8-14
©2002 Clint Harmon
THEN IT WAS DEBBIE!
Email: clintoons@aol.com
BUT THIS IS THE LAST STRAW!
TAP! TAPPITY! TAP!

SIGH! IT'S JUST LIKE WORLD WAR 2!
WHAT IS?
9/15-21
THIS STRICT DIET THAT I'M ON ...
©2002 Clint Harmon Email: clintoons@aol.com
TO FIGHT THE BATTLE OF THE BULGE!

I SEE YOU'VE ALMOST FINISHED YOUR BOOK!
NOT REALLY! I ALWAYS READ THE LAST CHAPTER FIRST!
9/22-28
WHY?
BECAUSE I LIKE HAPPY ENDINGS!
©2002 Clint Harmon Email: clintoons@aol.com
IF I'M GOING TO BE DISAPPOINTED. IT'S GOING TO BE BEFORE I READ 400 PAGES!

THIS SOUP IS THIN AND DOESN'T HAVE MANY NOODLES!
©2002 Clint Harmon Email: clintoons@aol.com
WHOA! MAN, I'VE GOT TO QUIT THINKIN' OUT LOUD!
9/29-10/5
BUT THAT'S JUST THE WAY I LIKE IT!
?

HAH! WHO SAYS YOU CAN'T TAKE IT WITH YOU?
©2002 Clint Harmon
10/6-12
YOU NOT ONLY CAN, BUT, ...
... YOU HAD BETTER!
YOU MUST TAKE IT WITH YOU BY ORDER OF: PARK POLICE
PARK DOG TRAIL
Email: clintoons@aol.com

YOU GOT MAIL
WOW! 38 E-MAIL MESSAGES!
NO KIDDING, WHO FROM?
©2002 Clint Harmon
Email: clintoons@aol.com
ONE FROM YOUR AUNT FLO, ONE FROM UNCLE OBIE!
AND THIRTY SIX FROM MOM WITH CUTE BABY PICTURES ATTACHED!
10/13-19

SNAKE!!
SNAKE!!
CHOP!
CHOP!
?
10/20-26
THAT DOES IT! YOU'RE GETTING NEW GLASSES!
Email: clintoons@aol.com
YOU JUST KILLED OUR NEW GARDEN HOSE!
PUFF!
PUFF!
WHEEZE!
©2002 Clint Harmon

GOOD MORNING!
HOW ARE YOU TODAY?
10/27-11/2
Email: clintoons@aol.com
DID YOU SLEEP WELL LAST NIGHT?
HOW'S TH' WIFE AND KIDS?
©2002 Clint Harmon
DON'T YOU JUST LOVE TH' NEW USER FRIENDLY COMPUTER SOFTWARE?

IT'S GETTIN' LATE, MAY I USE YOUR PHONE?
YOU BET. USE THE ONE IN TH' HALL!
OH DRAT! I CAN'T USE THIS PHONE!
HEY UNCLE OBIE!
I DON'T HAVE TH' RIGHT CHANGE!
NO PROBLEM!
©2002 Clint Harmon Email: clintoons@aol.com

HAVE YOU HEARD TH' SAYIN' "THERE'S MORE THAN ONE WAY TO SKIN A CAT"!
YUP!
WELL, RIGHT NOW...
I'LL SETTLE FOR TH' ONE WAY!
PRRRR! PURR!
©2002 Clint Harmon Email: clintoons@aol.com

LET'S WEIGH, I WANT TO CHECK ON YOUR DIET PROGRESS!
UH, OH!
I ONLY HAVE ONE QUARTER!
©2002 Clint Harmon
Email: clintoons@aol.com
11/17-23
OH WELL, WE CAN WEIGH TOGETHER!
THAT WON'T WORK!
SURE IT WILL, WE'LL JUST DEVIDE TH' TOTAL BY TWO!
weigh
25¢

WE ARE THANKFUL FOR OUR FIRST YEAR OF WEDDED BLISS!
WE ARE THANKFUL THERE'S STILL HOPE FOR GRANDCHILDREN!
I'M THANKFUL FOR MY SENIOR CITIZEN DISCOUNT CARD!
I AM THANKFUL THAT THERE WILL BE LEFTOVERS
I WILL BE THANKFUL WHEN THEY ALL LEAVE!
11/24-30
©2002 Clint Harmon
Email: clintoons@aol.com

WOW! YOU SHOULD GO DUCK HUNTING WITH ME KEN!
ZING!
BAM!
PING
GEE! I DON'T KNOW DAVE!
IT'S JUST LIKE **SKEET SHOOTING** THOSE **CLAY PIGONS**, ONLY MORE FUN!
Email: clintoons@aol.com
©2002 Clint Harmon
GEE, I NEVER THOUGHT ABOUT IT THAT WAY! **YEP, I'LL GO!**
OH NO! JUST WAIT TILL IT DAWNS ON HIM THAT THOSE **CLAY PIGONS** WILL BE REAL LIVE **DAFFYS N' DONALDS!**
12/1-7
CONTINUED

WELL DAVE, DUCK HUNTIN' HAS BEEN GREAT SO FAR, BUT I HAVE ATE TH' LAST **JELLY DONUT** AN' FINISHED TH' **HOT CHOCOLATE!**
12/8-14
©2002 Clint Harmon
SO. WHEN DO WE START HAVIN' FUN?
ANY MINUTE NOW!
Email: clintoons@aol.com

60

HERE THEY COME!
WHAT AM I DOING HERE? THESE DUCKS HAVE NEVER DONE ANYTHING TO ME!
12/15-21
©2002 Clint Harmon
SPLAT!
ARRG!
Email: clintoons@aol.com
UNTIL NOW!
BLAM! BLAM!
BLAM!
CONTINUED NEXT WEEK

?
!
BLAM!
BLAM!
BLAM!
12/22-28
KEN, WHAT HAPPENED? YOU'RE A CRACK SHOT AND YOU MISSED EVERYTIME?
NEXT WEEK KEN HAS BIG NEWS!
©2002 Clint Harmon Email: clintoons@aol.com
THOSE WERE WARNING SHOTS! IT'S ONLY FAIR!
REVOKE HIS DUCK HUNTING LICENSE!

FOLKS, THERE'S GOING TO BE A LITTLE **ADDITION** TO **OUR FAMILY!**
IF I'M DREAMING, DON'T EVER **WAKE ME!**
OH NO IT'S TOO **CROWDED** AROUND **HERE NOW!**
Happy Holidays
12/29-1/4
©2003 Clint Harmon Email: clintoons@aol.com

CARL, YOU WON'T HAVE TO PICK KEN UP TODAY!
WHY? WHAT'S WRONG?
HE JUST FOUND OUT HE'S GOING TO BE A DADDY!
HE'S A LITTLE UP IN TH' AIR TODAY, BUT HE SHOULD BE **SETTLED DOWN** BY TOMORROW!
?
1/5-11
© 2003 Clint Harmon E-mail: clintoons@aol.com

PRAISE BE! WE'RE GOING TO HAVE A GRANDCHILD. WHAT MORE COULD WE POSSIBLY ASK FOR?
CLANK!
©2003 Clint Harmon Email: clintoons@aol.com
1/12-18
TWINS!
www.rimrockcanyon.com Dist.By Clintoons Features

WE WERE JUST THINKING HOW WONDERFUL IT WOULD BE TO HAVE TWIN GRANDCHILDREN!
1/19-25
ONE GIRL!
ONE BOY!
©2003 Clint Harmon Email: clintoons@aol.com
TELL THEM THAT
THIS ISN'T A DRIVE THROUGH ORDER WINDOW!
www.rimrockcanyon.com

OOW! MY STOMACH IS REALLY GIVING ME A BAD TIME!
TAKE SOMETHING!
DARN DIET!
©2003 Clint Harmon
Email: clintoons@aol.com
WHAT?
OH, WHATEVER SEEMS TO HELP AT A TIME LIKE THIS!
www.rimrockcanyon.com
Dist.By Clintoons Features
THAT'D BE A BACON CHEESEBURGER!
1/26-2/1

OH TO RELIVE THOSE GOOD OL' DAYS!
GREAT MEMORIES EH, UNCLE OBIE?
2/2-8
©2003 Clint Harmon Email: clintoons@aol.com
YOU BET!
www.rimrockcanyon.com Dist.By Clintoons Features
INSTEAD OF FIFTEEN PERCENT, YOU COULD SQUEAK BY ON A FIFTEEN CENT TIP!

OH HONEY, THE FLOWERS ARE JUST LOVELY, BUT...
2/9-15
Dist.By Clintoons Features
www.rimrockcanyon.com
I'M REALLY SORRY ABOUT THE CANDY! I HAVE TO WATCH MY DIET DURING MY PREGNANCY!
©2003 Clint Harmon Email: clintoons@aol.com
NOT TO WORRY! WASTE NOT, WANT NOT!
KEN'S DIET R.I.P.
RIGHT ON DAD! TOSS ONE OVER HERE!

YOU NEED EXERCISE JOSE!
FETCH!
!
2/16-22
www.rimrockcanyon.com Dist.By Clintoons Features
WELL!
©2003 Clint Harmon Email: clintoons@aol.com
I DON'T DO STICKS!

ZZZ
THEY SAY CATS SNEAK UP AN' STEAL PEOPLE'S BREATH WHILE THEY SLEEP!
©2003 Clint Harmon
2/23-3/1
I DON'T GET IT! BUT BEING A CAT I'M JUST CURIOUS!
Email: clintoons@aol.com
GAG! YAK! YOU CAN KEEP IT! GARLIC BREATH!

PLEASE GIVE MY COMMENTS TO YOUR CHEF!
HEH, HEH! YOU MEAN COMPLEMENTS!
3/2-8
www.rimrockcanyon.com Dist.By Clintoons Features
NO! I MEAN COMMENTS!
©2003 Clint Harmon Email: clintoons@aol.com
TELL HIM HIS DISHWATER IS BEGINNING TO TASTE A LITTLE LIKE SOUP!

OOOH! ME! I'M CALLING IN SICK TODAY!
WHY HON? WHAT'S WRONG?
©2003 Clint Harmon Email: clintoons@aol.com
Dist.By Clintoons Features
THIS SUSPENSE IS KILLING ME!
www.rimrockcanyon.com
IT'S ABOUT 175 DAYS TILL OUR BABY ARRIVES!
HEY! I'M THE ONE THAT'S PREGNANT!
3/9-15

MOM, DAD, PLEASE FORGET ABOUT TWINS, I DON'T WANT YOU TO BE DISAPPOINTED!
OH, WE'RE NOT FOCUSING ON TWINS ANYMORE!
©2003 Clint Harmon Email: clintoons@aol.com
NOT AFTER THAT WONDERFUL DREAM I HAD LAST NIGHT, FROM NOW ON ...
Dist.By Clintoons Features
www.rimrockcanyon.com
IT'S TRIPLETS!
3/16-22

MR. FIGWELL, WHAT SINGLE THING DO YOU THINK HAS ATTRIBUTED MOST TO YOUR LONG AND EVENTFUL LIFE?
3/23-29
www.rimrockcanyon.com Dist.By Clintoons Features
THAT'S EASY LARRY!
BREATHING REGULARLY!
©2003 Clint Harmon Email: clintoons@aol.com

WHERE'S DA LEAK?
CHUCKLE HEH. HEH!
ACE PLUMBING
CHUCKLE! DO YOU MIND IF I ASK YOU A PERSONAL QUESTION? HEH. HEH!
3/30-4/5
©2003 Clint Harmon Email: clintoons@aol.com
WHERE'S CURLEY AN' LARRY?

WE'RE SO THRILLED ABOUT BEING GRANDPARENTS THAT WE JUST CAN'T WAIT FOR THE BABIES TO GET HERE!
4/6-12
DAD! I WAS HOPING YOU TWO HAD GOTTEN OVER YOUR OBSESSION ABOUT A PLURAL PREGNANCY!
OK.OK. BUT I STILL HOPE YOU GUYS HAVE GROUP INSURANCE!
www.rimrockcanyon.com Dist.By Clintoons Features
©2003 Clint Harmon Email: clintoons@aol.com

BE REALISTIC FOLKS, YOU'RE GOING TO HAVE ONLY ONE GRANDCHILD!
TIME WILL TELL!
©2003 Clint Harmon Email: clintoons@aol.com
YOU BET IT WILL, LIKE TOMORROW!
WHEN I HAVE TH' ULTRASOUND SCAN!
4/13-19

BOY! OUR "ALL YOU CAN EAT SPECIAL" HAS REALLY PACKED THEM IN TONIGHT!
YEAH BUT...
OUR PROFIT MARGIN JUST TOOK A DIRECT HIT!
4/20-26
©2003 Clint Harmon Email: clintoons@aol.com

WELL! JUST LET ME TELL YOU WHAT I THINK ABOUT THAT! UNCLE OBIE!
NOW, NOW, MY DEAR!
YOU ARE MUCH TOO YOUNG TO KNOW WHAT YOU ARE TALKING ABOUT!
©2003 Clint Harmon
4/27-5/3
Email: clintoons@aol.com
WELL! I HAVE NEVER BEEN SO DELIGHTFULLY INSULTED IN ALL MY LIFE!

WELL, HOW DID TH' ULTRASOUND SCAN GO? WHAT'S TH' GOOD NEWS ON TH' POSSIBILITY OF TWINS?
www.rimrockcanyon.com Dist.By Clintoons Features
LET ME PUT IT THIS WAY, I'VE GOT GOOD NEWS AND BAD NEWS!
©2003 Clint Harmon Email: clintoons@aol.com
5/4-10
GOOD NEWS FOR ME! BUT BAD NEWS FOR YOU!
IT'S A SINGLE OCCUPANCY!

YOU DIDN'T TAKE OUT TH' GARBAGE!
I DON'T GET IT! HOW COME THAT'S ALWAYS MY RESPONSIBILITY?
5/11-17
©2003 Clint Harmon Email: clintoons@aol.com
WELL! I GUESS YOU DIDN'T READ TH' SMALL PRINT!
SMALL PRINT? WHERE?
www.rimrockcanyon.com Dist.By Clintoons Features
ON TH' APPLICATION YOU FILLED OUT FOR OUR MARRAGE LICENSE!

IF KNOWING WHAT YOU KNOW NOW, AND YOU COULD LIVE YOUR LIFE OVER, WOULD YOU DO ANYTHING DIFFERENTLY?
5/18-24
©2003 Clint Harmon Email: clintoons@aol.com
YOU BET I WOULD!
www.rimrockcanyon.com Dist.By Clintoons Features
THIS TIME AROUND I COULD CORNER TH' STOCK MARKET!

THE NOBLE DOG, EVER VIGILANT IN PROTECTING THE HOUSEHOLD!
5/25-31
ROAR! RUMBLE! KABLAM! CRASH!
©2003 Clint Harmon Email: clintoons@aol.com
I WONDER WHO I TENDER MY RESIGNATION TO!

©2003 Clint Harmon
HOLD STILL!
?
6/1-7
Email: clintoons@aol.com
THERE!
OUR BABY IS NOT DUE FOR MONTHS, BUT TH' OL' MOTHERING INSTINCT HAS ALREADY KICKED IN!

HONEY, I DON'T CARE IF OUR BABY IS A BOY OR GIRL, AS LONG AS IT'S HEALTHY,
©2003 Clint Harmon Email: clintoons@aol.com
HAS A HIGH IQ, BIG BLUE EYES, CURLY BLOND HAIR,
www.rimrockcanyon.com Dist.By Clintoons Features
6/8-14
AND LOOKS EXACTLY LIKE ME!

YOU'RE MY GREAT, GREAT UNCLE BUT, JUST HOW OLD ARE YOU?
GO FIGURE! I REMEMBER ROOSEVELT'S TIME!
OH, WHEN FRANKLIN ROOSEVELT WAS PRESIDENT?
NO! THEODORE!
6/15-21
©2003 Clint Harmon Email: clintoons@aol.com

I HEARD SOMEWHERE THAT AN UNBORN CHILD CAN HEAR VOICES!
I JUST WANT YOU TO KNOW THAT I'M TRULY SORRY...
...FOR WHAT I SAID THIS MORNING AFTER THROWING UP!
© 2003 Clint Harmon
E-mail: clintoons@aol.com
6/2-28

AW, COME ON DEB, I WANT TO SEE HOW THIS MOVIE ENDS!
© 2003 Clint Harmon
É-mail: clintoons@aol.com
6/29-7/5
NO! IN MY CONDITION I'VE GOT TO GET TH' RIGHT AMOUNT OF SLEEP!
WHAP! WHAP! WHAP! WHAP! WHAP!
OK YOU GUYS, GO AHEAD AND KEEP ME AWAKE NOW!... BUT MY DAY IS COMING!

WOW, DEB. ALL THESE CHORES ARE GETTING ME DOWN!
7/6-12
DON'T COMPLAIN TO ME. I'M DOING MY PART...
...BABY SITTING!
© 2003 Clint Harmon E-mail: clintoons@aol.com

YOU LOVE DOGS SO MUCH UNCLE OBIE, WHY DON'T YOU GET **ONE OF YOUR OWN?**
©2003 Clint Harmon Email: clintoons@aol.com
WHEN JOSE MISSES TH' PAPER WHO GETS TH' **DODO DUTY?**
ER, UH, ME OR **DEB!**
I THINK YOU JUST **ANSWERED** YOUR **OWN QUESTION!**
7/13-19
www.rimrockcanyon.com Dist.By Clintoons Features

TOUCH DOWN!
I THINK OUR BABY WILL MAKE A GREAT **FOOTBALL PLAYER!**
7/20-26
©2003 Clint Harmon Email: clintoons@aol.com
WHY DO YOU **SAY THAT?**
I THINK HE JUST **KICKED** A **FIELD GOAL!**

HONEY, I HAVE BOTH **BAD AND GOOD NEWS** TODAY!...
7/27-8/2
THE BAD NEWS IS I BACKED INTO ANOTHER CAR BUT...
THE GOOD NEWS IS MAMA IS COMING TO STAY TILL AFTER THE BABY ARRIVES.
I LIKE **TH' BAD NEWS BETTER!**
© 2003 Clint Harmon E-mail clintoons@aol.com

FIRST TIME PARENTS SEMINAR
TODAY WITH TH' AID OF OUR LITTLE DOLL WE WILL DEMONSTRATE TH' FINE ART OF **DIAPER CHANGING!**
8/3-9
www.rimrockcanyon.com
©2003 Clint Harmon Email: clintoons@aol.com
PSST; **WOW**; TALK ABOUT ***REALISM!***
TEE HEE. ***PEANUT BUTTER!***

BETTY GOT ONE. NADINE GOT ONE AND CAROL GOT ONE!
?
©2003 Clint Harmon
Email: clintoons@aol.com
BUT TH' BOSS WON'T LET ME HAVE ONE!
ONE WHAT?
8/10-16
www.rimrockcanyon.com
MATERNITY LEAVE!

NURSE, IS MY UNCLE OBIE BUSY?
YES, HE'S TAKING HIS UPPER BODY EXERCISES
ISN'T HE A LITTLE TOO OLD FOR THAT?
NO! NOT REALLY!
©2003 Clint Harmon Email: clintoons@aol.com
IT'S VIDEO GAMES!
8/17-23

DAD. MOM. WHAT WOULD YOU LIKE FOR YOUR ANNIVERSARY GIFT??
YOU ALREADY HAVE IT ON ORDER DEAR, AN' WE'RE JUST WAITING ON DELIVERY!
8/24-30
WE HAVE ??
SURE! IT WAS ORDERED MONTHS AGO! "OUR GRANDCHILD!"
©2003 Clint Harmon Email: clintoons@aol.com

IF IT'S A BOY MAYBE HE'LL FULLFILL MY LIFELONG DREAM AN' BECOME A FAMOUS BASEBALL STAR!
8/31-9/6
IF IT'S A GIRL! MAYBE SHE'LL FULLFILL MY LIFELONG DREAM...
www.rimrockcanyon.com Dist.By Clintoons Features
©2003 Clint Harmon Email: clintoons@aol.com
...BY BECOMING THE COUNTRY'S FIRST WOMAN PRESIDENT!

KEN! KEN! WAKE UP!! I WANT YOU TO GO AND GET ME SOMETHING!
9/7-13
©2003 Clint Harmon
AN ICE CREAM SUNDAE, TOPPED WITH OLIVES AN' CATSUP!
Email: clintoons@aol.com
BUT IT'S TWO A.M.!
YUMMY! BUT HOLD TH' OLIVES AN' CATSUP!

I FEEL YOUR PAIN! HERE'S SEVENTY FIVE CENTS! KNOCK YOURSELF OUT!!
HAD NO COFFEE TODAY PLEASE HELP!
9/14-20
HEY! SEVENTY FIVE CENTS! I'LL NEED THIRTY BUCKS!
OF COURSE, THAT INCLUDES TRANSPORTATION ACROSS TOWN TO MY FAVORITE ESPRESSO!!
HAD NO COFFEE TODAY PLEASE HELP!
©2003 Clint Harmon
Email: clintoons@aol.com

NO. NO. PRINCESS!
9/21 - 27
MY **LAP** IS OCCUPIED NOW!
?
THAT'S KID'S GONNA BE **TOUGH COMPETITION!** HE'S NOT EVEN HERE YET AN' HE'S ALREADY A **LAP** AHEAD OF ME!
©2003 Clint Harmon Email: clintoons@aol.com
www.rimrockcanyon.com
Dist.By Clintoons Features

JUST LOOK AT THAT! HE'S ALWAYS HAD **ONE!**
10/15 - 18
NOW SHE HAS **ONE TOO!**
©2003 Clint Harmon Email: clintoons@aol.com
THEY WOULDN'T HAVE THOSE STOMACHS, IF THEY'ID TOSS **MORE UNDER TH' TABLE!**
THE **BABY** IS DUE **SOON!**

OUR BABY IS DUE SOON, WHEN WILL YOUR MOTHER BE **FLYING IN ?**
??
10/19 - 25
©2003 Clint Harmon Email: clintoons@aol.com
YOU KNOW VERY WELL THAT MOTHER WOULD NEVER SET FOOT ON A PLANE! SHE TO **AFRAID TO FLY!**
PLANE? HE MEANT **BROOMSTICK!**

WHOA!
?
10/26 - 11/1
...LOOK AT THIS E-MAIL **FROM MOM AN' DAD!** THEY WANT TO COME OVER **EVERY NIGHT...**
©2003 Clint Harmon Email: clintoons@aol.com
TO HOLD AN ALL NIGHT BABY WATCH VIGIL, TO MAKE SURE YOU GET TO THE **HOSPITAL IN TIME!**

WAKE UP, KEN! WAKE UP!
OK! OK! LAST TIME IT WAS A "SUNDAE WITH CATSUP AN' A OLIVE"! SO, WHAT'S IT GONNA BE NOW?
11/2-8
© 2003 Cloint Harmon E-mail: clintoons@aol.com
WELL, I PERFER A GIRL BUT TESTS INDICATE ONLY A 50/50 CHANCE!
NOW GET UP! WE'RE GOING TO TH' HOSPITAL!

WHAT ARE YOU DOING? GET READY TO GO TO THE HOSPITAL!
11/9-15
©2003 Clint Harmon Email: clintoons@aol.com
YOU'LL SEE! I'M ACTIVATING MY PREARRANGED...
BABY ALERT SYSTEM!
BABY ALERT SYSTEM??
DON'T MISS NEXT WEEK!

THEY'RE HERE!
UNCLE OBIE'S STORK EXPRESS!
11/16-22 © 2003 Clint Harmon E-mail: clintoons@aol.com

WOW! DO THEY MAKE THIS MUCH FUSS OVER EVERYONE WHO HAS A BABY!
HEH! HEH!
© 2003 Clint Harmon E-mail: clintoons@aol.com
NOT UNLESS THEY HAVE AN UNCLE OBIE WITH CONNECTIONS AT CITY HALL!
EEEEEEEEOOO
ZOOM!
SEE YOU AT THE HOSPITAL NEXT WEEK!
11/23-29

DON'T WORRY DEB, I'LL BE RIGHT HERE WITH YOU **ALL TH' WAY!**
11/30-12/6
© 2003 Clint Harmon E-mail:clintoons@aol.com
WOW! INVOLVED IN TH' BIRTH OF MY OWN **OFFSPRING!**
REALLY WANT TO BE INVOLVED? TRADE PLACES **WITH ME!**

DELIVERY
WOW! NOW THAT HAS TO BE SOME KIND OF RECORD, THEY **JUST TOOK HER IN!**
12/7-13
© 2003 Clint Harmon E-mail: clintoons @aol.com
www.rimrockcanyon.com

SO YOU'RE TH' TENDERFOOT THAT JUST ARRIVED! AROUND HERE I'M KNOWN AS "TH' OL' TIMER"
12/14-20
www.rimrockcanyon.com Dist.By Clintoons Features
WOW! HOW LONG YOU BEEN HERE?
!
I RECKON IT'S BEEN NIGH ON TO TWELVE HOURS NOW!
©2003 Clint Harmon Email: clintoons@aol.com

WHO COULD BE CALLING AT 3 A.M.?
RiNG!
12/21-27
DAD! DO I HAVE A GREAT CHRISTMAS GIFT FOR YOU! "A GRANDSON"!
©2003 Clint Harmon Email: clintoons@aol.com
WHAT IS IT?... A TORNADO OR AN EARTHQUAKE?
NEITHER, IT'S A BOY!
Happy Holidays to you and yours!